STEVE HEUZINKVELD

RAIDERS OF THE FALL

THE FALL SERIES BOOK TWO

Dedicated to my Oma, Lena Heuzinkveld.
Thank you for igniting my passion for books.

Gone, but never forgotten.

Foreword

While this story is based on real locations throughout the United States, I have used fictitious names for some towns and neighborhoods, so that I can change certain aspects of these locations for the sake of the story.

Thank you, and enjoy!

CHAPTER 1

"Who the hell could've done this?" Hayden Marsh put their thoughts into words, covering his nose with the collar of his undershirt as they crept through the eerie streets of the forever-silenced small town.

"I thought this place was supposed to be safe," Chelsea Preston shrank away from the bullet-riddled bodies strewn across the sidewalks, fighting the urge to gag.

"We should get back to the truck," Katanya Grady checked their rear with a sweep of her hunting rifle, making sure that their escape route was still clear. "Whoever did this might still be hanging around."

"I don't think so," Riley Armstrong held her father's pistol up as she led the way. "Whoever did this, it was a big group. We would've seen somebody by now."

Despite her confidence, Riley still stopped short of every store window and open door, glancing at the empty shelves and overturned offices inside before resuming their steady advance up Clementine's Main Street.

She stepped over a familiar dead body as they passed by a brick-lined bank.

It was the same greasy mechanic who would wolf-whistle at her every time they came into Clementine to trade.

The mechanic – along with countless others – had been running from whoever had stormed the town. Riley could tell by the bullet spray across the brick wall and the bloody streak that he had left along the pavement, crawling half a dozen yards towards whatever he thought could have saved him.

Evidently, he had thought wrong.

"Don't tell me we're still looking for batteries," Katanya spoke softly from the rear of their single file formation along the sidewalk.

"Where else are we gonna find them?" Riley glanced back at the other three. She jerked her head towards the town's main intersection, "Herb's diner's just up ahead. Let's head there first and then we'll check the store."

Pressing her shoulder into the bricks of a building, Riley scanned the corner on the other side of the street, checking for any signs of movement.

With her forefinger laid alongside her pistol's trigger guard, she swept the gun's barrel back across the road, before edging out from behind the corner.

Broken bottles and scorch marks blotched the intersection. Glass crystals twinkled in windswept piles underneath the shattered windows of the diner.

"Herb!" Riley called across the desolate street. She knew that she was giving away their position, but she'd rather have a shootout with hostiles before engaging in friendly fire. "We're coming over!"

She gazed back at her three companions with bated breaths, waiting for the man's neighborly acknowledgment that never came.

Herb was being cautious.

He had to be.

There was no doubt in her mind that the portly man was watching them from one of the second-story windows above the diner, with his double-barrel shotgun tracing their every move.

Ruddy streaks flowed down the diner's steps onto the pavement like a rusty red carpet that abruptly ended at the curb.

The front door had been kicked off the hinges, hanging ajar at an odd angle, solely suspended by a twisted scrap of metal in the doorway.

Riley peered inside through the broken entrance, with Hayden backing her up on the steps while Katanya and Chelsea warily glanced up and down the ghostly intersection.

Lead pellet craters pockmarked the diner's walls, surrounded by copper red sprays and splotches of blood. Spent shotgun shells and a windswept stack of table napkins littered the floor. Splintered strips of wood hung from the booths where bodies had fallen backwards onto the tables, although there were no signs of the raiders' carcasses now.

The small bell above the diner's entrance gave a mournful chime as Riley shouldered the stubborn door open, the hanging frame scraping noisily along the floor.

Behind the counter, surrounded by empty boxes of ammo, with one hand eternally reaching up for one of the few remaining bottles of liquor on the top shelf, Herb's body was draped unceremoniously over the sink with a hole in the back of his head.

Riley's pupils dilated at the sight of the slumped diner owner.

She had only known the man for a few months, but he had

been the community's lifeblood – the reason why most of them had even lasted this long after the apocalypse.

And now he was dead, along with the rest of Clementine's townsfolk.

"Check the back," she glanced sidelong at Hayden before walking the length of the diner, sweeping each booth to make sure that they were truly alone before jumping behind the counter.

With a strained grunt, Riley heaved Herb's body from the sink, sending his stiffened corpse to the floor with a hollow thud.

Swallowing the lump building in her throat, she rolled him onto his back with the heel of her sneaker and forced herself to look down.

Despite the violence of his death, the big friendly owner of the diner had died grinning. With windows shattering around him, bullets flying overhead and the raiders kicking down his door, Herb had been in the midst of his last stand, defending Clementine to his final breath.

Riley crouched beside him, her fingers moving to close his lifeless eyelids, when she drew her hand away, flinching at the thought of touching him, afraid that she would disturb his rest and contort his smiling face into something far more sinister.

"Looks like they cleaned house," Hayden emerged from the kitchen, stopping short of Riley and Herb as he surveyed the grisly scene behind the counter. "Place is empty."

"Did you check upstairs?" she peeled a sticky bar mat off the counter and knelt down again to lay it over Herb's head – hardly the shroud that the man deserved, but better than what he had been given.

"Yeah," Hayden frowned as he stared up at the bottles of

4

liquor on the top shelf. "They even took the mattresses off the bed frames." He stepped over Herb's body to reach up for an expensive-looking bottle of bourbon before glancing back down at Riley. "Dunno how the hell they missed this though."

Riley cocked her head in contemplation, her gaze flicking over towards the other bottles remaining on the liquor rack, when a pair of footsteps scuffed across the pavement towards the diner's entrance.

CHAPTER 2

Riley's heart skipped a beat.

Staying low behind the counter, she seized a handful of Hayden's shirt and yanked him down to the floor beside her.

Raising a finger to her lips, she swung her pistol up, keeping the gun's barrel just below the edge of the counter.

"Guys?" Chelsea Preston's voice broke the tension as the blonde college girl appeared in the diner's doorway. "You might wanna come check this out."

Hayden snorted sidelong at Riley's edginess.

She threw him a warning glare, stifling his smile in an instant.

Riley refused the offer of his firm helping hand as they rose to their feet again, leaving Herb's corpse behind the counter and heading back outside.

Katanya was standing opposite a row of bodies lined up along the side of the general store across the intersection. Taking her eyes off the carcasses, the ebony sentinel looked through the scope of her hunting rifle, keeping tabs on their black crew cab pickup parked behind the town's makeshift barricade in the distance.

"They executed all the men," Chelsea explained, whispering over her shoulder as they crossed the street, as if she was afraid that the sound of her voice might wake the dead.

Sure enough, the sheriff and his deputies were heaped across the pavement, along with some of the local farmers who had flocked to Clementine for the false promise of safety in numbers. The three Bradford Brothers lay side by side with the local barber and a slew of other vaguely-familiar faces that Riley had sometimes glimpsed on their trips into town.

But not one woman was lying among the row of bullet-riddled cadavers.

The mothers and the waitresses and the schoolteachers turned sentries had all disappeared, leaving the once peaceful small town deathly silent.

"I don't have to say what we're all thinking," Hayden supposed, still holding the expensive-looking bottle of bourbon as he glanced around at the other three. "About what happened to the women, I mean."

"Can we leave now?" Chelsea asked in a small voice, looking over her shoulder.

"I agree," Katanya waved off a corpse fly before raising her eyebrows at Riley. "We're not safe here."

"We need those batteries," Riley jerked her head towards the row of bodies as a reminder, "Now, more than ever. Hayden, you check the store. Katanya, keep an eye on the truck, we're not staying long. Chelsea, with me."

They were reluctant to follow her instructions, but they followed her all the same.

They didn't really have much of a choice.

Riley always kept the keys to the truck in her pocket whenever they made a supply run.

The three of them had left her stranded without a vehicle in the past, and part of her would never forgive them for it, in spite of how close they had grown to each other over the past few months.

Shards of glass crunched underfoot as Hayden disappeared into the shadowy general store, while Katanya retreated halfway back towards their truck, leaning her shoulder against a telephone pole as she scanned up and down Main Street.

Chelsea simply stood in stunned silence, watching as Riley crouched to pat down the dead sheriff and his deputies. The sheltered college girl had been taken care of by her brother and their friends ever since their chaotic exodus from the West Coast. There had never been a need for her to get her hands dirty.

For Riley though, this wasn't the first time that she'd had to search a corpse.

"What are you looking for?" Chelsea clapped her hands over her mouth as the wind changed, turning her face away from the wafting reek of sickly-sweet rotten meat, struggling to swallow her nausea.

"My dad was a police officer," Riley gritted her teeth as she moved on to the next body. "If anyone's got spare batteries for a walkie, it's these guys."

The sheriff and his deputies had already been stripped of their kit belts, but she was hoping to find a set of keys. Maybe they could search the locker room of the sheriff's office, or there might have been a forgotten stash in one of the patrol vehicles shoring up the makeshift barricades along the outskirts of town.

"What about the Bradfords?" Chelsea suggested as she stepped out into the street, trying to escape the pervading stench of the rotting carcasses.

Riley had half a mind to call the balking blonde back over to search their bodies for herself, but she wasn't completely convinced that Chelsea would be thorough enough.

With the last of the deputies' pockets proving fruitless, Riley squatted beside the three Bradford Brothers. She had no idea what their first names were, but together, they had been responsible for running Clementine's cluster of camping, hunting and fishing stores.

"Good thinking," Riley admitted as she pulled a set of blood-encrusted keys from the first brother's jeans.

Just as she was getting back onto her feet, a wooden *clack* pierced the silence of the macabre massacre, echoing from the barricaded extremities of the small town.

CHAPTER 3

"Katanya, did you hear that?" Riley pulled Chelsea around the corner back onto Main Street, unintentionally squeezing the set of keys into the supple flesh of her upper arm.

Chelsea gasped in pain and snatched the keys out of Riley's hand, before gasping again at the sight of the dried blood smeared across the jingling shrapnel.

"Yeah, I got nothing though," Katanya Grady called back from farther down the street, scanning the distant barricade behind them with a sweep of her hunting rifle. She glanced back over her shoulder at their truck before covering them again. "Come away from the intersection."

Chelsea's sneakers scuffed the pavement as she took off running back towards Katanya, checking the indents on her arm as she went.

"Hayden, let's go!" Riley whispered a shout into the shadows of the general store as she shrank backwards along the sidewalk.

Gripping her pistol with both hands, Riley arced the gun's barrel from side to side between the corners of the crossroads with her forefinger laid alongside the trigger guard.

She had no idea which way the sound had come from, but one thing was for certain – they weren't alone.

"What's going on?" Hayden ambled out of the general store, the big brawny idiot casually strolling straight into Riley's line of sight. He held up his hands in surrender, swinging his bottle of bourbon aloft. "Whoa, whoa, what's happening?"

"Fucking hell – move!" Riley jerked her pistol back over to the far side of the intersection, only for Hayden to hurry past the gun's barrel again.

She exhaled in exasperation before resuming her steady retreat, sweeping the crossroads and occasionally glancing back over her shoulder, making sure that she wouldn't stumble over one of the bloody corpses strewn across the sidewalk.

"Where the hell's Chelsea?" Riley glanced around when they caught up to Katanya.

"Probably back at the truck by now," she lowered her hunting rifle as she and Hayden turned to jog along the pavement towards their black crew cab pickup in the distance.

Biting her bottom lip, Riley took cover behind a telephone pole, warily watching the intersection, her pulse pounding as she waited an eternal minute for the other two to climb back over the town's makeshift barricade.

"Let's go, Riley!" Katanya finally shouted from the pickup's tray, staring down the sights of her hunting rifle resting on the roof of the truck's cabin.

"Shit, hold on!" Hayden's voice rose up from behind the town's vehicle blockade.

Riley wasn't planning on waiting around for him to elaborate.

She turned away from the intersection and bolted down the pavement, still cradling her pistol in both hands as she kept the barrel pointed at the curb.

GUVV!!

Katanya's hunting rifle woofed a finger of hot lead overhead, ripping through the air towards the crossroads.

"MOVE, MOVE, MOVE!!" she yelled from the back of the pickup, lining up another shot.

Icy adrenaline ran through Riley's veins as she ducked her head down into her chest, keeping her gaze locked on a white post van backed up against the barricade.

GUVV!!

She didn't dare look back over her shoulder to see whoever Katanya was shooting at, but *cracks* of gunfire erupted from somewhere behind her in response, bullets zipping by and punching holes into the vehicle blockade just up ahead, shattering headlights and windscreens in the lead shower.

Riley's legs were churning towards the front of the parked van, her knees coiling into springs, ready for launch, when a streak of gold flashed in front of her.

It was too late to stop.

She surged straight into the sudden obstacle with enough force to send them both crashing into the front of the van.

"Chelsea, what the fuck!?" Riley wheezed against the post van's dust-caked grille, all of the air knocked out of her lungs.

Bleeding from a fresh gash above her temple, Chelsea sat up in a daze, her eyes swimming with shock and confusion as she stared sidelong at Riley.

Another barrage of bullets brought them both back to life, hot slugs pinging off metal and crunching through wood.

Chelsea scrambled up onto the van's hood while Riley whirled around to return fire.

Her vision was swimming as she fought to win back her

breath, but she could just make out a man garbed in green crouching for cover in the entrance of the brick-lined bank.

The pistol barked in her hands as she laid down suppressing fire for Chelsea to make her clumsy escape.

Her bullets went wide, but considering the distance, combined with her stilted breathing, hitting the barred windows and the sign above the bank's entrance was better than she could have hoped for.

The white post van creaked behind her as Chelsea jumped over the barricade.

GUVV!! GUVV!! GUVV!!

"Riley, come on!!" Katanya roared over rapid fire rifle rounds, pinning down whoever was on their tail.

Lurching to her feet, Riley took a fleeting moment to flip the safety lever on her pistol before clambering up the front of the van, still struggling to reel in ragged breaths as she climbed up the windscreen, her sneakers squeaking and streaking across the glass.

More gun blasts echoed from the heart of Clementine as she crawled across the roof of the van, splinters of wood exploding from the makeshift barricade mere inches from her face.

Her heart drumming in her ears, Riley lunged headfirst over the scraps of wood and metal lining the vehicle blockade, landing in a crumpled heap on the other side.

Katanya's hunting rifle surrendered with an impotent *click*, and the ebony sentinel slung the spent smoking barrel over her shoulder before leaping down from the truck's tray, rushing around the black crew cab pickup to haul Riley up onto her feet.

"Move your fucking legs, bitch!" Katanya clenched her jaw as she half-supported, half-dragged Riley's leaden body back towards the truck, more bullets biting through the barricade behind them.

"Keys, keys, keys!!" Hayden roared as soon as Katanya threw the back door open, his outstretched hand shaking as he ducked low in the driver's seat.

Riley shook herself out of her stupor for long enough to toss him the car keys and fling herself up into the cabin, with Katanya shoving her along the backseat to climb in after her.

"Shit!" Katanya pulled her hand back from the open door as the window exploded into glass crystals.

"Just leave it open!" Chelsea screamed from underneath the glove box as the engine rumbled to life, blood glistening from the gash above her temple running down her cheek.

"How many of them are there!?" Hayden stomped on the accelerator and wrenched the steering wheel around, tires screeching as they mounted the curb before taking off down the highway.

"Fucking hell!" Katanya ducked low as the rear window shattered next, glancing sidelong at Riley as they breathed hard in the backseat. She shook her head in disbelief as she met Hayden's gaze in the rearview mirror, "I only saw one guy."

CHAPTER 4

They took the long way back to the farm just in case they were being followed – even though gas wasn't exactly a resource that they could afford to spare, especially now.

Apart from the batteries, this was supposed to have been a routine supply run. Trading their excess game meat for candles, toiletries and a closely-monitored ration of fuel had become a regular part of their lives over the past few months.

Under Herb and a few other key influential members of the close-knit community, Clementine had been the central hub for bartering resources between all of the fledgling settlements surrounding the small town.

But not anymore.

Riley supposed that it was only a matter of time before the people of Nebraska began taking rather than trading.

"That's the best I can do until we get back," Katanya studied the wrap around Chelsea's head before settling into the backseat again.

She had bandaged the wound with a torn strip of her own shirt, which was really Riley's shirt, since the three young women had been sharing the clothes out of her suitcase ever since they had arrived at her grandmother's farm.

"Thanks," Chelsea glanced up at her reflection in the vanity mirror before looking away, cringing at the sight of her own blood soaking through the cloth. At least her wound had begun to clot.

"What the hell were you doing?" Riley sat up on the floor mat draped over the backseat, the broken glass crystals crunching underneath. "You had a head start on the rest of us. Why weren't you already back in the truck?"

"I was looking for the batteries," Chelsea squirmed around in the front passenger seat, patting her pockets.

"Did you get them?" Hayden stared sidelong at her before remembering that he was supposed to be driving. It was his first time behind the wheel in months.

"No, I forgot which size we needed," Chelsea confessed, although she was wearing an expression of relief rather than regret. "But I found something better in the Bradford Brothers' back room."

She withdrew a black and yellow walkie from the pocket of her pink track pants, gazing back at Riley and Katanya with a victorious smile – the facial movement immediately causing her to wince in pain.

"Does it work?" Riley reached for the two-way, her eyebrows raised.

The radio spoke for itself as she thumbed the power button, studying the set of numbers and symbols flickering to life across the small display screen. Having experimented with their pair of police radios in the early days of the apocalypse whenever they went out on hunts and supply runs, the Bradford walkie was far more user friendly in comparison.

Riley spun the volume dial and clicked through some of the

channels before switching the radio off again, acutely aware of its batteries being down to their last third of juice.

"Should we call them?" Chelsea glanced at each of them in turn, her eyes soon settling on the truck's stereo.

"Not until we get back," Riley gazed out the window at the picturesque countryside sailing by, absent-mindedly adding, "Good job, guys."

Checking out of the conversation, she lost herself to the landscape, watching the rolling fields and forests of Nebraska rise and fall, the peaceful autumn vista occasionally broken by the dirt ribbon of a rutted farm road or a rustic homestead standing sentinel in the distance.

The serene scenery reminded her of all the interstate trips that her family had taken to visit her mother's relatives in years gone by. A younger version of herself would sit in the backseat of their red suburban, with Nolan Armstrong behind the wheel, and her mother, Susan, by his side, pointing out the passenger window as she relived memories of her own childhood.

Riley couldn't help but think about how her whole world had been turned upside down ever since the day that they had left Redhurst for the last time.

But then again, so had everyone else's.

Aside from her own group's struggle to survive during the advent of the apocalypse, she had overheard several grim snippets of just how far civilization had sundered circulating around the townsfolk of Clementine.

Kidnappers and scavengers had laid claim to the freeways.

Entire convoys and campgrounds were being set upon by raiders down south.

And in the east, windswept clouds of radiation were devouring everything in their path, sentencing any survivors to agonizing weeks of withering decay, before deciding to grant themselves the mercy of death.

The long list of lost loved ones grew every time another travel-worn batch of ragged refugees came through town, seeking sanctuary from the fallout that had ravaged the rest of the country.

And with every new person came some new piece of information that would always spill over into speculation.

Everybody had their own theories as to how and why the asteroid had changed its trajectory upon entering the atmosphere, arguing their conflicting scientific opinions to the point of ad nauseam.

But as much as their theories about the asteroid differed, there was always one thing that they could all agree on – the complete lack of an appropriate military and governmental response.

After the coordinated effort to silence the spread of panic over the approaching asteroid, the falsely-projected impact site of the asteroid itself, along with the half dozen missiles that had completely missed their mark with devastating results – it was as if all of the politicians had gone into hiding, with every last one of them utterly unwilling to accept any form of responsibility, or even at the very least, provide a road to recovery.

In spite of everything – without access to any official aid or assistance – Riley and her group had still managed to eke out a modest existence for themselves, relying on their trades with the close-knit community of Clementine for any resources that had been outside of their reach or skill set.

But now, they were on their own.

Well, not exactly.

The raiders who had destroyed the entire town were still roaming around Nebraska.

CHAPTER 5

A sudden lurch and rumble pulled Riley Armstrong out of her reflection, and she was sitting in the backseat of the black crew cab pickup again.

They trundled down the dirt road of her grandmother's farm, dry autumn leaves clinging to the trees lining the driveway on either side. The waters of the small reservoir shimmered on the paddock in the distance as the evergreen pine forest stood tall behind the big weatherboard home.

Susan Armstrong stood with her arms folded on the wooden veranda alongside Greg Preston, keeping watch, as they always did whenever Riley and Chelsea went into town without them.

"Who wants to tell them what happened?" Hayden asked as they pulled up next to Aunt Lorraine's blue farm truck, glancing sidelong at the bloody makeshift bandage wrapped around Chelsea's head.

"I'll do it," Riley took a deep breath at the sight of her mother venturing down the veranda's steps.

Steeling her resolve to be the bearer of bad news, Riley popped the door handle and shouldered it open, but before she could jump down onto the grass, a shout went up from the veranda.

"Chelsea!?" Greg ran across the yard towards his sister as soon as she opened the front passenger door. Red rage and white fear splotched his face as he stared at the dried blood down her cheek in bewildered fury. "Tell me who the fuck did that."

Riley bit her bottom lip as she sized up the ropey blonde.

He was usually laid-back and friendly – a typical Californian beach boy – but he was the polar opposite whenever it came to his sister's safety.

And Riley had just bowled her over headfirst into the front of a post van.

She swallowed her uncertainty.

There was no point hiding the truth.

"It was me," Riley confessed, hopping out on the other side of the pickup alongside Hayden. "It was her own fault though."

"Are you fucking kidding me?" Greg stared daggers at Riley through the truck's cabin. "How would you like it if I –"

"Can everybody just relax for a second?" Katanya swung her door out wide and climbed down beside Greg, partially fencing him off with both of the open doors.

"I jumped out in front of her," Chelsea admitted, placing a soothing hand on her brother's shoulder. "It was an accident."

"Fucking better have been," he shot a warning glare at Riley before helping his sister out of the truck, "Come on, let's get you cleaned up."

"Bring her to the bathroom," Katanya unslung the empty hunting rifle from her shoulder as she followed the pair of siblings towards the veranda. "We need to wash the wound before I can bandage her up properly."

"Greg," Susan shot him a stern sidelong stare as the three of them passed by. "Don't you ever swear at my daughter again."

He held her cautionary gaze, swaying on his feet as he considered issuing her a warning of his own, before Chelsea began urging her slighted brother up the veranda's wooden steps.

The screen door banged open just as they reached the top of the stairs.

"What the fuck have you done to my truck!?" Keith Bowman shoved his way past Greg, the broad-shouldered police officer's stony eyes glowering at the broken windows and bullet holes. "Riley, you better have a fucking good explanation!"

Susan threw up her arms in frustration, shaking her head behind Keith as he strode past to assess the damage.

Hayden stood dumbstruck beside Riley at the rear of the pickup as the rest of their friends disappeared into the house. He was holding the car keys in one hand and the expensive-looking bottle of bourbon in the other.

Subtly, he tried to pass the keys back to her, wincing as the little pieces of metal betrayed him with a slight jingle, earning himself the spotlight of Keith's fury.

"Don't tell me you got drunk and used my truck for target practice," Keith held Hayden square in his death stare, clenching his jaw as he summoned every ounce of restraint.

"What? No, I – we…" Hayden trailed off, wilting under the man's glare and shrinking closer to Riley.

"You… cock-sucking butt-plugging shit-chugging pillow-fucking…"

Riley's first instinct was to cut across Keith, but she was at a loss for words, awestruck by the sheer extent of the whiskey-cured man's vulgar vocabulary. She could almost see the steam blowing out of his ears as he reeled off the articulate string of profound profanity.

"… wart-licking dick-sitting ring-rimming finger-sniffing…
"

Susan struggled to stifle a smirk as she locked eyes with her daughter, equally impressed by Keith's eruption of seemingly endless insults. Having been cooped up in Grandma Eleanor's house for months on end with a firm filter on his foul language had certainly taken its toll on the man.

"… pinecone in a sandwich and go fuck yourself with it!" the ridges of Keith's frown began to smooth as he heaved a heavy sigh of cathartic release.

"Are you done?" Susan raised her eyebrows behind him. "You haven't even given them a chance to hear their explanation."

Having sworn himself into silence, Keith turned away from Riley and Hayden, breathing deep and exhaling in contentment as a sense of calm and clarity washed over him.

It was as if an unbearable weight had finally been lifted from his shoulders.

He hadn't realized how much he had missed speaking his mind.

"I'll let you talk to them," Hayden handed the car keys over to Riley with a wary glance at Keith. "I should probably go."

"Yeah, that pinecone's not gonna fuck itself," Riley chuckled behind him, Hayden's feet faltering as he climbed up the veranda's steps.

"Riley, language," Susan chided, although she was unable to hide her smile this time. She nodded towards the truck. "Now would you mind telling us what happened?"

For a moment, Riley had forgotten all about the raid on Clementine, the townsfolk lying dead in the streets, and the

23

lone gunman garbed in green who had been hell-bent on adding her and the others to the body count.

She gazed back over her shoulder, narrowing her eyes at the highway on the horizon.

CHAPTER 6

"I need to see it for myself," Keith Bowman hooked his thumbs into his belt loops, his stony gaze flicking between Riley and Susan.

The former policeman struck an imposing figure, with his broad-shouldered silhouette framed by the sun's westward descent, his beefy frame stretching Nolan Armstrong's fur-lined leather aviator jacket to its absolute limits.

Riley was still unsure about how she felt every time she saw Keith wearing one of her father's outfits. Part of her wished that Keith had brought an extra backpack of his own clothes for their one-way interstate road trip to Nebraska – after all, he had packed almost everything else.

The other part of her was relieved to see that he was still keeping her father's memory alive – whether Keith knew it or not – and she could think of nobody else more worthy of wearing his wardrobe. Thankfully, Hayden, Greg and Jesse had found better fitting clothes in the gray motorhome parked out back with the other vehicles.

"No, you don't," Susan swept the last of the broken glass crystals from the back of the black crew cab pickup into a dustpan. "That madman could still be hanging around, and from the sounds of it, we're lucky that Riley and the others are still alive. Who knows? Maybe he killed the whole town single-handedly."

"Maybe, but the only way we'll know for sure is if I go," the likely lingering danger didn't daunt Keith in the slightest. If anything, he was emboldened by it. "I hope that shooter's still hanging around by the time I get there," he nodded at the plethora of craters pockmarking his truck. "I need to get his insurance details. Can't buff this shit out."

He turned to Riley with a slight smirk, holding his hand up for the car keys.

Standing by the pickup's rear wheel, Riley cocked her head to one side, undecidedly fidgeting with the keys before glancing over at her mother.

"Just what exactly do you need to prove?" Susan shut the rear passenger door and drew up beside her daughter, pursing her lips at Keith from the other side of the truck's tray. "This isn't a murder investigation. It's not a manhunt. There's no justice system for whatever happened to those people. Why does it matter if you go?"

"We need to know what we're up against," Riley answered for him, her gaze going from Keith to Susan, "And we should find out what happened to all the women."

"That's right," Keith nodded his appreciation at her taking his side.

He looked pointedly at the car keys again, still holding his hand up expectantly.

"But you'd be taking a risk that could get you killed," Riley decisively handed the keys over to her mother, Keith's short-lived relief dropping from his face as fast as his arm fell to his side. She leaned over the pickup's side rail to emphasize her next point, "Or worse, he could follow you back here and kill the rest of us."

"I'd be careful," Keith argued indignantly, eyeing the pair of women. "I could bring Katanya with me. She's good with that rifle."

"She was with Riley when they ran into him," Susan raised her eyebrows at him as she pocketed his keys before nodding towards the truck's shattered rear window, as if he needed a reminder. "And look how that turned out."

"Then I won't bring her," he shrugged, going straight back to Plan A. "Doesn't change a thing. I still need to see Clementine. It'll help me do my job here."

"Just how exactly would leaving the farm help you protect it?" Susan narrowed her eyes at him, searching for the sense in his argument.

"If I can see what happened to them," he began, his stubbled square jaw set with stubborn determination, "I'll know what to look for so the same shit doesn't happen to us."

Riley shook her head, exhaling at his bullheadedness and glancing back at her grandmother's big weatherboard home.

She furrowed her eyebrows at the sight of someone's silhouette standing just behind the screen door, eavesdropping on their conversation.

"*We* saw Clementine," Riley reasoned, turning back towards Keith. "Why can't you just ask *us* what you need to know?"

Keith sucked his front teeth and stared up at the darkening sky.

He knew that he wouldn't be able to win against the mother and daughter team.

Their arguments were both sane and sound, and all he

wanted to do was get off the farm for a while.

He felt like a big dog that hadn't been let loose for the longest time.

Tasked with patrolling the property's perimeter while enduring his son's unrelenting resentment for months on end, he just wanted to take a break from it all – even if that meant driving straight into a shootout.

Letting out a heavy sigh, he nodded in resigned silence at Riley and Susan.

Satisfied, the two women turned back towards the house while Keith reached into the back of the pickup to lift the cooler out – still filled with the frozen cuts of excess game meat that they had intended on trading for their next fortnight's worth of supplies.

Lorraine Tipton held the screen door open wide as they shuffled inside. From behind her thick glasses, her beady eyes crawled over the shape of Keith's body underneath the fur-lined leather aviator jacket, switching between his pair of beefy arms and lingering, as if she wanted him to catch her staring.

Now that Riley was eighteen years old, it hadn't taken very long for her to finally understand why her father had never been able to patch things up with her aunt.

If nothing else, the matronly woman was unwaveringly persistent.

Only a few weeks after the asteroid and the half dozen misguided missiles had wreaked havoc across the nation, Keith had made the mistake of playing along with one of Lorraine's bawdy probes, jokingly agreeing that they should all play a part in repopulating the country.

And ever since that rueful night, she had taken every opportunity to get her claws into him, caking her face with makeup and shamelessly putting herself on display, clutching to a thin hope that his will would eventually break and he would finally give in to her unreciprocated advances.

"Such a shame about your truck," Lorraine twirled a greasy brown lock of her hair as Keith came in through the door. "I can give you the keys to mine, if you like. I'll need help finding them though. Meet me in my bedroom after dinner?"

Riley stifled a snort and paused in the doorway to the living room, wanting to hear how the rest of their conversation would play out.

Susan, on the other hand, silently skirted around the staircase to make her way towards the kitchen, looking for Grandma Eleanor.

"Put this back in the meat freezer," Keith stiffly handed Lorraine the cooler, completely ignoring her thinly-veiled offer.

"Your wish is my command," she mewled as she unnecessarily groped his hand. "I'll take your meat wherever you wanna put it, Officer Bowman."

As if she wasn't being obvious enough, Lorraine shot him a pronounced wink before whirling away towards the kitchen.

Keith clenched his fists to ward off a shiver of disgust.

For a moment, Riley thought that he was going to punch a hole in the wall, but he must have felt her eyes on him.

Taking a deep breath to recompose himself, he slid the parlor room's door open and stepped inside, slamming it shut behind him.

Grandma Eleanor's weatherboard home was big, but it hadn't been built to house ten people.

Aunt Lorraine had her own bedroom, as did Susan. Katanya and Chelsea had taken the guest room that Riley used to sleep in as a child whenever her family came to visit. Riley herself had taken to alternating between sleeping beside her mother and her grandmother, both of them happy for the company.

The boys had gotten the raw end of the deal though.

Hayden and Greg had laid claim to the gray motorhome parked out back – and they were welcome to it, both sets of its previous occupants having met grisly ends.

That left the old couches in the parlor room to Keith and Jesse, although they seemed to take the room in turns. Jesse couldn't stand being around his father. He couldn't stand being around any of them.

"Are you coming or going?" Hayden called from the living room, sprawled out on a recliner in front of the TV that no longer worked.

"Sorry," Riley rubbed the back of her neck in the doorway, both her palm and her nape clammier than she would have liked. "I've just got a lot on my mind."

"Clementine, right?" Hayden supposed, weighing the expensive-looking bottle of bourbon in his hand, "Same here. I thought that place was gonna ride this whole thing out. Couple more months, government gets back on its feet, and we all go our separate ways."

"You and me both," she glanced at the liquor. It looked like an oversized bottle of perfume. It also looked like he hadn't opened it yet. She smirked at him, "Are you old enough to be carrying that around?"

"Older than you," he dodged the question with a hint of alarm in his eyes.

"You know there's a cop in the house, right?" she teased him, jerking a thumb over her shoulder.

"I don't think he's too concerned about underage drinking,"

Hayden grinned back at her.

Riley's smile faded.

She knew that he was talking about Jesse.

"I'm sorry, I didn't mean –"

"Forget it," she cut across his attempt to apologize, looking back over her shoulder. "You just – shut up. Stay here."

Riley crossed the hall, her sneakers squeaking over the parquetry as she approached the parlor room.

She rapped the sliding door twice with the back of her hand.

"Fuck off, Lorraine!" Keith's whiskey-cured voice growled over the sound of a shotgun cocking a shell into the breech. "How many times do I have to tell you!? I'm not fucking interested!!"

"It's Riley," she sidestepped away from the door, just in case he didn't believe that it was actually her.

"Fuck me – come in," Keith grunted, cocking the shotgun a few more times to cycle through the rounds, clearing the chamber.

"Is she really that bad?" Riley asked as she slid the door open, her eyes falling to the shells rolling across the carpet.

"I'm just cleaning it," he offered an offhand explanation as to why he was holding his shotgun. Glancing around the room for a rag to support his claim, he shrugged before setting the gun down on the coffee table. "What's up?"

"I thought you'd have some more questions for me," she entered the room, walking across the cold fireplace's stone hearth to sit down in a cozy armchair, "About what we saw in Clementine."

"Alright," Keith settled back into the undersized couch that had doubled as his bed for the past few months. He stroked the stubble across his jaw, "What kinda ammo were they using?"

31

"The raiders or the gunman?" Riley cocked her head slightly, realizing that it wouldn't make much of a difference anyway. She didn't know the answer to his question either way. "Actually, I'm... not sure."

"You didn't see any shell casings?" he prompted, raising his eyebrows. "Maybe get a good look at some of the bullet holes?"

Riley's hazel eyes turned downcast, as if the answer was written somewhere across the well-worn carpet.

The only casings that she had seen were Herb's spent shotgun shells in the diner, although she hadn't exactly been searching for empty cartridges scattered among the bodies on the ground.

Her mind turned towards the bullet holes instead.

She had thought that they would have been easier to remember.

After all, every last man in town had been gunned down, and yet their bodies were as vague as the details of a dream.

Every time she tried to focus on the corpses strewn across the sidewalks, she could only see the blood soaking through their clothes and staining their horrified faces.

Despite their entire gory ordeal in the newly-established ghost town, there was only one hole that had managed to stay with her – the one that she had seen in the back of Herb's head.

"I don't think they were using shotguns," she finally answered, looking back up at Keith.

"Is that it?" he frowned, an air of impatience beginning to darken his face as twilight fell outside. "What about the groupings on the people who ran? Was it one shot, one kill? Or did they just spray and pray?"

"I – I wasn't paying attention," Riley fumbled for an answer, furrowing her eyebrows as she tried to conjure up an image of the greasy mechanic sprawled across the pavement outside the brick-lined bank. Unconsciously, her fingers began to fidget in her lap, and she felt as though she was being grilled in an interrogation room. She answered truthfully, "I can't remember."

"What about the bodies outside the general store?" Keith pushed his line of questioning, "Did they get mowed down? Or was it an execution?"

"Lighten up, Keith," Susan appeared in the doorway with an old brass candlestick, the small flickering flame bringing a warming glow into the shadowy parlor room. She pursed her lips as she slid the door shut behind her, "Why don't you try asking her about something else?"

"What's the point if she can't even remember?" he cast a frustrated hand at Riley. "That's it. First thing tomorrow, I'm going."

"You're asking her about a bunch of dead bodies," Susan shot a sympathetic glance at her daughter before turning towards Keith again. "Have you stopped to think that maybe she doesn't wanna remember?"

"Pretty crucial pieces of information," Keith muttered under his breath, making a conscious effort towards keeping a lid on his profanity.

"Why's that?" she set the brass candlestick on top of the cold fireplace's mantel before placing her hands on her hips. "What difference does it make how they died?"

"Because…" his stony gaze went from Susan to Riley and back again, softening as he recognized his former partner's family still soldiering on without their husband and father. He took a deep breath and exhaled slowly before taking on a gentler tone. "Knowing how they shoot tells us whether we're dealing with pros or amateurs. If they're spraying bullets, it means they've got automatics, they've got ammo to burn, and they're either sloppy or rushed."

Silence hung over the parlor room as Susan stooped to pick up Keith's shotgun shells. She placed them one by one on the coffee table, eyeing them both.

"They sprayed," Riley spoke up from the armchair, her memory becoming clear again as she took comfort in the tension leaving the room, "At the people who ran, and everyone outside the general store. Herb was probably the only person they killed with a single bullet – but not for lack of trying."

Keith nodded in silence, staring down at the shotgun shells on the coffee table.

"That's good, Riley," Susan stood and went to the windows next, drawing the curtains closed against the gathering dusk outside. "What else do you remember?"

"They cleaned out the diner," Riley narrowed her eyes at her recollection, "The kitchen. The mattresses upstairs. Even the salt and pepper shakers were gone."

"They can use the salt and pepper for food preservation," Susan nodded knowingly, moving to another window.

"But for some reason," Riley shook her head slowly, still trying to work it out herself, "They left all the alcohol behind."

"Did they touch the cash register?" Keith wondered aloud, staring up at the ceiling.

"I honestly can't remember if I saw it," Riley furrowed her eyebrows at him, "But nobody uses money nowadays. Why would that even matter?"

He sat forward on the couch for a long moment, rubbing his stubbled jaw as he silently digested all of the information.

With a wavering glance at Jesse's smaller sofa across the

room, Susan dusted off the sheet puddled at the end of Keith's makeshift bed, smoothing out the creases before taking a seat beside him.

"They're not just a bunch of amateurs," Keith concluded, looking up at them both. "Most of their shooters might be, but they've probably got a few pros keeping them all in line. They're focused, not impulsive. Taking what they need, and leaving what they don't."

"So, what should we do?" Riley's eyes went from her mother to Keith.

"Well, we've got a working walkie now," he settled back into his seat with a solemn look on his face. "Maybe we should contact whoever's been making those broadcasts. They might know something about the attack."

"You know how I feel about this," Susan folded her hands over the couch's armrest with a sigh, having already expressed her concerns over the looped message they'd all heard on the truck's radio. She made eye contact with Riley, shaking her head, "I was really hoping you wouldn't come back with the batteries."

"Looks like you got your wish," Riley gave her a small snort as she withdrew the black and yellow walkie from her jeans pocket. "Let's hear what the others think first though. Maybe they've changed their minds after today."

CHAPTER 7

"If there's anybody listening, my name is Braxton Shepherd...
I represent an organized group of survivors in Nebraska...
We've built up a safe community just outside of Burview... We
have food, water, shelter and medicine... We're opening up
our doors to anyone who's willing to earn their keep... We'll be
on channel four... Do not approach the radio tower without
calling ahead... I repeat – do not approach the radio tower
without calling ahead... If there's anybody listening..."

Riley had committed the looped recording to memory ever
since they had first heard the radio broadcast in the truck
during their last trip into town.

From the look on everyone else's faces as they filed into the
candlelit dining room, it seemed that the same message was
on the forefront of all of their minds as well.

"I thought we decided that we weren't going to call them,"
Grandma Eleanor sat at the head of the dinner table, her
wrinkled face bristling at the thought of being forced to leave
her home.

"What happened in Clementine changes things, Ma," Susan
ladled a spoonful of mashed potatoes onto her mother's plate

before passing the pot around.

"We can't hold out here for long without the supply runs," Keith explained from the opposite end of the table, as far away from Lorraine as he could get without leaving the dining room.

"Told you that place wouldn't last forever," Greg Preston leaned over in between Katanya and Chelsea, loading up his soup bowl before sitting down beside Hayden at the breakfast bar behind them.

Riley stirred the piping hot venison soup with her spoon, waiting for it to cool down as she sat in between her mother and the ever-empty chair that had been set aside for Jesse.

They had voted against the idea of making contact with Shepherd's group a fortnight ago. At five against four, Susan had negated the possibility of Jesse's absent vote from bringing them to a tie by reminding the four college students that they didn't have a working radio to contact Shepherd's people anyway.

Reluctantly, Greg had accepted the group's decision, provided that they added batteries to their shopping list on today's trip into town – just in case.

Ever since hearing those three prudent words, Riley had known that their resolution would be subject to a revote as soon as they returned with their haul.

But with Keith beginning to change his tune, it seemed that they no longer held the majority.

"*Supply runs,*" Eleanor Tipton scoffed at Keith with a dismissive hand wave, the elderly woman swelling with fiery grit as she stared around at them all. "None of you have ever lived through a war. Back when Nolan was still a twinkle in his father's eye, having candles and soap was a luxury. We never needed all that rubbish to get by."

"I'm... Keith," he clarified, his uncertain gaze sliding sideways towards Riley and Susan.

"I know," Grandma Eleanor scooped up a spoonful of mashed potatoes as she stared back at him across the length of the dining table. "Nolan wasn't such a pussy."

"Grandma!" Riley laughed along with the others.

"What?" she asked innocently, before remembering the rule against profanity that she had imposed on everyone else. "Well, it's my house, and I'll say what I damn well please."

"Pussy or not, he has a good point," Hayden scooted his chair backwards to turn away from his bowl on the breakfast bar. "If we can't get any more fuel for the truck and the generator, eventually we're all gonna be stuck here with spoiled meat in the freezer."

"We could trade with the neighbors," Lorraine spoke out of the side of her mouth as she chewed, not even bothering to turn around to make eye contact with Hayden. "Who knows? Maybe we could be the next center of commerce in Nebraska."

"That'd be like painting a target on your back," Katanya murmured beside her as she bent over her soup bowl.

"Yeah, how much do you trust your neighbors?" Greg piped up from behind them.

"I think they'd be more trustworthy than complete strangers," Riley furrowed her eyebrows at the blonde Californian beach boy. "For all we know, Shepherd's people might be the same group who attacked Clementine."

"I doubt it," he scoffed at the suggestion, although he had nothing else to say to support his claim as he silently turned back to his venison soup.

"You know, after what we saw today," Katanya kicked back her chair to look over her shoulder at Greg and Hayden, "You two should probably be more concerned about all this than us women. None of the guys we saw in town had a happy ending."

"Well, regardless," Chelsea spoke up on behalf of her brother, the wound on her head wrapped with an actual bandage now, "If we stay here, we won't be able to last the winter."

"Oh hush, child," Grandma Eleanor cooed reassuringly. "We have enough meat in the freezer to last until summer. And if we run out of fuel for the generator, then we can salt and smoke it all into jerky!"

"You can't eat jerky, Ma," Susan softly reminded her mother of her fragile dentures.

"And I can't eat meat," Chelsea reminded them all of her vegan diet.

"It's a wonder you've lasted this long," Lorraine snorted in amusement, glancing sideways at the sheltered college girl's plate of mashed potatoes and pine nuts.

"What about this," Hayden set aside his empty soup bowl and picked up his expensive-looking bottle of bourbon, finally cracking it open. "What if we just packed up everything here and drove down south towards the coast?"

"It'd be better than wintering here," Greg supposed, sliding his glass towards him across the breakfast counter.

"I don't think we have enough fuel to even make it outta Nebraska," Riley flicked her gaze between the two of them as Hayden filled Greg's glass. "And that's if we could all squeeze into the same truck. If we had to split up into two cars, we'd only get half as far."

She glanced over at her grandmother, and as lively and spirited as the old woman was, Riley knew that she wouldn't survive an interstate trip if they were forced to go on foot.

39

"Don't forget about all those raids on camps and convoys down south," Katanya reminded them of the stories that they had overheard every time a new group of travel-worn refugees came through Clementine. "I'd rather take my chances here with the winter."

"It's not so bad," Grandma Eleanor set her cutlery down with a satisfied smile, having spent more winters on her farm than any of them had seen in their entire lives. "Hot soup by the fire. Mulled wine for dessert. Speaking of which..." she gave Hayden a little wave, "Young man, bring that bottle over here and serve up some bourbon for the rest of us."

Aunt Lorraine was the first to down the water in her glass as Hayden circled around the dining table, the tension in the room beginning to subside as they all marveled at the top shelf liquor's smooth aftertaste.

Hayden paused beside Riley for a moment, giving her mother a wary glance.

Seeing the smiles surrounding them, Susan gave him a stiff nod of approval, but she placed her hand on his forearm before he could make it a double shot.

It wasn't Riley's first drink – that much was for sure, lifting the glass to her lips without hesitation – but it was certainly her first taste of top shelf liquor. It felt like a mouthful of sweet silk caramel gliding down her throat, a slow smile spreading across her face as she sighed at the velvety warmth mingling with the venison soup in her belly.

"Look, it all sounds good," Keith brought everyone straight back to business, "Buckling down here for the winter and roughing it out until it gets warm again... But think about what happened to Clementine for a second, with all their barricades and all their manpower and all their guns. If a place like that can go down – what chance do we have out here on a big open farm, with just the ten of us to hold it?"

A hush fell over the room, with only the occasional swallow of bourbon breaking the long silence as everyone pondered the likelihood of their own survival.

"We have to call Shepherd's people," Hayden concluded, settling back into his seat at the breakfast bar. "And we have to do it soon, because if we end up changing our minds after we're snowed in, or if we get hit by the raiders before then, it'll be too late for any of us to make the call."

"And what if Riley's right?" Susan stared at each of them in turn, "What if Shepherd's people were the ones responsible for what happened in Clementine? We'd be inviting the raiders right onto our doorstep."

"You got a better suggestion?" Greg knocked back what was left of his glass and poured himself another drink, "Preferably one that doesn't involve my sister getting sick off game meat and the rest of us having to live without soap for months on end."

Riley looked towards her mother, Grandma Eleanor and Aunt Lorraine, hoping that one of them would come up with a compromise that they could all agree on. Her optimism was short-lived though, the three women soon staring at one another with equally blank expressions.

"Well, guess we'll vote on it," Greg shrugged at their silence, glancing around at them all, "Two for calling – me and Chelsea."

"Three for calling," Hayden stared down at the breakfast bar's countertop, compelled to stand by his friends. He took a sip of his bourbon before the shadow of a smile creased the corners of his lips, "Greg smells bad enough *with* soap. Can't imagine him without it."

"I don't care what anyone else says," Grandma Eleanor's face wrinkled with resolve, "I'm not going anywhere. This is my home, and I'm going to die here. Alone, if I have to."

"I'm staying too, Ma," Susan placed a gentle hand on her mother's arm. Glancing sidelong at Keith with a tear rolling down her cheek, she added, "I trusted the wrong people last time, and we lost Nolan for it... I'm not leaving my family for a bunch of strangers."

"Three for staying," Riley spoke over the sound of her mother's soft sobs. She shot a hard stare at Keith, determined to bring him back over to their side. "We went through hell and back just to get here – I'm not risking everything we sacrificed just because these guys want some fucking soap."

"Language, dear," Grandma Eleanor smirked as she took another sip of bourbon.

"FOR FUCK'S SAKE!!" Keith slammed his fist down on the dining table, cutlery and dishes jumping as everyone jolted upright in their seats. He clenched his jaw at Riley and Susan, seething at their stunned silence. "If you stay here, you'll die. Winter's gonna get you girls killed. If the cold doesn't do it, the raiders will. You start a fire, and they'll see the smoke coming from the chimney. And after the shit I've seen with all my years on the force, you'll wish you were dead after what they do to you."

"Then we'll use blankets to keep warm," Grandma Eleanor swelled in defiance, speaking on behalf of her family at the head of the table. "There's more than one way to drive out the cold, young man. And you'll learn that faster than it'll take for winter to get here if you keep up that tone in my house."

"Fine," he muttered, downing the rest of his bourbon and

swallowing his anger. Wiping his mouth with the back of his hand, he looked over at Riley and Susan again. "I've kept you both safe this far. I've done right by Nolan. You wanna risk your lives by staying here, that's on you. But not me, and not my boy. We're leaving."

Riley exchanged a glance with her mother, but it seemed that there was nothing that either of them could say to convince him otherwise.

"Katanya?" Hayden prompted through the hush that had fallen over the room.

"Four," Katanya locked eyes with Riley across the table, "For staying."

"*Staying!?*" Chelsea echoed beside her incredulously, gazing back at her brother to check whether she had heard her correctly. She leaned closer to Katanya, dropping her voice, "Didn't you hear what Keith just said? Death by the cold, or death by the raiders. What part of that gives you the impression that you've got a better chance here?"

"I made my vote," she cocked her eyebrow at the blonde college girl. "Deal with it."

"And I thought Chelsea was the one who hit her head," Greg snorted from the breakfast bar behind them. His lips moved wordlessly as he glanced around the room, silently adding up the votes. His eyes settled on the back of Lorraine's chair, and his cocky smile fell from his face. He gulped audibly. "Maybe we should wait for Jesse."

"He didn't vote last time," Riley answered quickly, having come to the same realization of who held the majority. "I don't see why that should change now."

"Five," Aunt Lorraine paused for a moment to savor every-one's attention, her thick glasses gleaming in the candlelight as she gazed around at them all. She propped her elbow up on the table and leaned to one side, biting her pinkie's fingernail as she turned to smile at Keith, "For calling."

CHAPTER 8

Riley Armstrong silently crept into her mother's bedroom, only to find that the sheets were empty.

She had been certain that after the long night spent arguing in the candlelit bowels of the big weatherboard home, her mother would have wanted nothing more than to stay in bed until at least midday.

After all, Susan had been adamant that she wanted no part of whatever was going to happen in the morning, when Keith was supposed to make radio contact with Braxton Shepherd's people.

Despite the hours and candles that they had spent debating around the dining table, no amount of bargaining or reasoning had swayed the outcome of the vote. In fact, the one and only thing that they had all managed to agree on was that they should arrange the meeting with Shepherd's group closer to Clementine, and far away from the farm.

As strong as their resolve had been, Keith and the others couldn't deny the need for a backup plan, just in case things went south.

Their shared fleeting moment of fearing the unknown alone

should have been enough to make them second-guess their decision, but by that point, Riley couldn't have cared less whether they stayed or went.

She just wanted to be sure that her family would be safe.

In the darkness of her mother's bedroom, Riley pulled on a pair of faded denim jeans and a gray hoodie before venturing downstairs, her path lit by the early morning rays of pale sunlight streaming in through the window above the wooden staircase.

She was on the bottom step when a faint creak sounded from behind.

Her heart rate spiked, and an unbidden image of the lone gunman garbed in green flashed across her mind's eye.

On instinct, she grabbed hold of the handrail's pillar and swung herself around, only to stare up at the empty flight of stairs.

Certain that she had heard something though, she backpedaled away from the staircase, her sneakers squeaking over the parquetry of the hall as she glanced from side to side.

To her left stood the parlor room's closed sliding door, with Keith Bowman's occasional chainsaw-like snore rumbling from the other side.

To her right was the open doorway to the living room, still wreathed in shadows with the curtains drawn shut.

A hint of movement in the darkness snapped her gaze towards the outline of the recliner, and a cold finger sent shivers down her spine.

Shaking off the sudden chill, she crept closer to the living room, pausing at the doorway to let her eyes adjust.

Peering into the gloom, she could make out the silhouette of a solitary figure swaddled in blankets on the chair.

"Chelsea?" Katanya croaked uncertainly, the whites of her eyes blinking as she stirred.

"Shhh," Riley raised a finger to her lips as another faint creak came from somewhere around the corner.

Her sneakers whispered over the well-worn carpet as Katanya quietly drew back the blankets in her wake, easing herself out of the recliner to shadow Riley along the wall.

Their ears pricked up at the soft sounds of rustling and rummaging emanating from the kitchen.

The supplies, Riley realized, bristling as she pressed her shoulder into the wall and scanned around the corner.

Early morning sun rays spilling in through the kitchen's window fell across the dining table, shedding light on the waxy remains of last night's candles.

Just out of sight, they heard the pantry door gently swinging shut, as if it had been muffled intentionally, and a shadow swept over the dining room's floor.

Riley glanced back at Katanya, and she offered an iron-jawed nod in response, ready to confront the thief.

They rounded the corner, Riley with her palms raised like a pair of coiled vipers, while Katanya seized one of the brass candlesticks from the dining table – which she dropped the moment they laid eyes on the breakfast bar.

Arrayed across the countertop was a frying pan, the last of their vegetable oil, a glass jar, and a big battered mortar and pestle.

"Mom?" Riley uttered, both surprised and stupefied as her arms fell to her sides.

"Oh!" Susan turned around, holding a bag of pine nuts. "I'm sorry, I was trying not to wake anyone. How was your sleep?"

"Are you... cooking right now?" Riley furrowed her eyebrows as she pored over the utensils again, her adrenaline dissipating in shakes and jitters.

"I woke up craving something dipped in nut butter," she confessed with a guilty smile before shaking the bag of pine nuts. "I'm thinking maybe raw carrots, or –"

"Stress baking," Riley shook her head with a smirk as she sat down behind the breakfast bar to get her heart rate back under control. "I should've known."

"Do you need a hand?" Katanya offered, picking up the pestle.

"Sure, I just need to roast the nuts first," Susan chirped happily as she crossed the room towards the back door. "I've already got the fire going. Could you grab the frying pan? Riley, bring the radio."

Finding the black and yellow walkie behind the bottle of vegetable oil, Riley followed them outside, her breath frosting in the early morning autumn air.

Grandma Eleanor's backyard had always been Riley's private little playground whenever her family came to visit from California.

It was like a park without limits, stretching as far as the evergreen pine forest in the distance and beyond, unbroken by any fence line or barriers to keep the local wildlife at bay.

Filling the space in between was the old farm shed that had fallen into disrepair from decades of disuse, the vegetable garden that they had carefully rationed out over the past few months, and the various vehicles that had survived the interstate trip from Redhurst.

Immobile in the dewy overgrown grass, the weather-worn cars stood in the yard like mournful monuments to their dead and rotting owners. Sinclair's stately white coupe, Shaun's orange vintage muscle car, Bobby's old rust-bucket sedan, and the nameless occupants of the gray motorhome that Hayden and Greg had laid claim to.

Riley's shoulders shook with a shudder – and not from the cold – as their shoes crunched through windswept piles of golden leaves towards the gravel square beside the barn.

As promised, strips of kindling were crackling underneath the grill of the stone barbecue, their flames licking at the logs. The pinewood gave off blissful heat and a crispy sweet aroma as the three women warmed their hands by the fire.

"Shouldn't Keith have the walkie?" Riley wondered aloud as her mother poured half the bag of pine nuts into the frying pan.

"Probably," Susan gave the pan a shake to level out the nuts. "But I'm still undecided on whether I wanna break the radio and bury the batteries where no one can find them."

"Everyone knows you have it," Katanya reminded her as she sidled closer to the flames. "Besides, they're gonna make contact with Shepherd's people one way or another. No use in us burning bridges with them now... Not while they could still come back to tell us the place is safe."

"Is that why you voted with us last night?" Riley stepped away from the grill and tucked her hands under her arms, bracing against the cold. "Let the others risk their lives to test the water before you take the plunge?"

"Girls," Susan interjected, pursing her lips as she turned her head between the two of them. "I have a feeling it's gonna be a long winter, and I don't want us having a falling-out before it even starts."

"No, it's okay," Katanya nodded respectfully at Riley's question, despite the underlying implication. "I voted with you because I thought we'd win. I'm just trying to make the best of a bad situation."

"Sorry, I just…" Riley bit her bottom lip, searching for the right words. She didn't even know why she had snapped at her. Katanya had been nothing short of invaluable over these past few months, and for some odd reason, she had chosen Riley's family over her own friends. Riley leaned against the stone barbecue with a sigh, "I'm sorry. We're going from ten people to four after today… My aunt really fucked us, huh?"

Susan raised her eyebrows as she stared down at the frying pan, wordlessly humming her agreement.

"To be honest, I liked Hayden's suggestion better," Katanya paused to enjoy the earthy aroma wafting up from the roasting pine nuts, "The ten of us trying to make a play for the coast. It'd be tough going, and we'd be more exposed, but I have an aunt in the military based at Fort Morwell down in Texas. If we could make it there, I know she'd take care of us."

"But you said you'd rather take your chances with the winter," Riley furrowed her eyebrows. "Why didn't you bring this up last night?"

"Because it's too dangerous along the freeways right now," Katanya met Riley's gaze, reminding her exactly how they all first met on the road to Nebraska. "I'd prefer to wait until spring. Besides, we've got food, water and shelter here. We don't need to take the risk."

"Well, at least we've got the option," Riley supposed, watching as her mother removed the frying pan from the grill. "Don't get me wrong – I like it out here, but I don't wanna be stuck on this farm forever."

"I hear you," Katanya agreed with a glance over her shoulder at the big weatherboard home. "No offense, Mrs Armstrong, but this can't be it for us. I'm happy to stay here for the meantime, but we've gotta find our way back into civilization one day."

"Believe me, I get it," Susan rested the pan on the barbecue's stone ledge, the roasted pine nuts quietly crackling as they cooled. She chuckled to herself, "I remember when I first met Nolan. He said he thought everyone in Nebraska were just a bunch of paranoid hill folk who didn't take too kindly to strangers. He couldn't wait to whisk me away."

"You never told me that story," Riley looked sidelong at her mother, sharing her grin.

"Come on, I'll tell you inside," Susan picked up the frying pan again, the three women turning back towards the house. "And hand the walkie over to Keith. There's no point in us holding onto it now. I have a feeling we're gonna be just fine without them."

Riley withdrew the black and yellow walkie from her jeans pocket as they stepped off the gravel and onto the grass, the dew already beginning to melt in the pale morning sun.

Still smiling, she thumbed the radio's power button, just to be sure that her mother hadn't buried the batteries after all.

"… I say again," the two-way crackled. "This is Braxton Shepherd. We're parked on the road at the top of the driveway. All clear for us to approach?"

CHAPTER 9

"You snuck into my room!?" Susan Armstrong was upstairs, but her voice reverberated around the entire weatherboard home and out into the yard, rousing everyone from their sleep. "I can't believe you, Lorraine!"

"I had to!" her sister yelled back, "You heard Ma. She's not coming unless we force her to come. This is how we all stay together! This is how we stay alive!!"

The kitchen's back door creaked open.

With a jolt of dread, Riley whirled around, expecting to see Shepherd's people sneaking up behind her and Katanya.

"That smells amazing," Hayden Marsh appeared in the doorway, walking into the kitchen with Greg Preston in tow. They ogled the bed of roast pine nuts cooling in the tray on the countertop. "Thanks for making breakfast."

"Yeah, I didn't think we'd get a decent send-off after last night," Greg shoveled a handful of nuts into his mouth. He cocked an ear up at the ceiling as the screaming continued, "Sounds like they're still going at it."

Riley was about to tell the two boys that the pine nuts weren't for them, but she imagined that making nut butter would be the last thing on her mother's mind when she came back downstairs anyway, especially with Braxton Shepherd waiting outside.

Don't burn bridges, don't burn bridges, she reminded herself.

"Sure you haven't changed your mind?" Chelsea asked Katanya as the blonde college girl came in through the hallway, seating herself next to the tray on the breakfast bar.

"Guess we don't really have a choice now, do we?" Katanya fumed, glancing sidelong at Riley.

"This is bullshit," Riley glared at the other three with cold accusation in her eyes. "You guys were meant to meet up with Shepherd in Clementine."

"Not our fault," Greg shrugged, nut flecks flying from his mouth. "Your aunt made the call, apparently, not us."

She exhaled in exasperation.

Biting her tongue, she pushed past the Californian beach boy to grab a fistful of roast pine nuts before leaving the kitchen, chewing in resentment as her sneakers squeaked over the parquetry of the hall.

Pausing at the foot of the staircase, she could hear her grandmother's soothing voice floating down from the corridor upstairs, Grandma Eleanor doing her best to placate her two daughters.

Swaying on her feet, Riley teetered on the edge of racing up the staircase.

She wanted nothing more than to shove her aunt up against a wall and berate her for broadcasting their position, putting them all in danger.

But with a deep breath, she turned away from the stairs, crossing the length of the hall to punch the screen door open instead.

53

Riley stepped outside onto the veranda, joining Keith Bowman behind the wooden balustrade.

The former policeman had taken a liking to her father's fur-lined leather aviator jacket, his thick fleece collar turned up against the chill of the morning. He grunted a greeting before throwing a pointed glance at his shotgun propped up on the floor, hidden behind one of the wooden railing's pillars.

Taking care not to knock the weapon over, Riley peered up the length of the driveway to see an idling livestock truck parked in the middle of the highway in the distance.

"You got the walkie on you?" Keith grumbled in his whiskey-cured voice, eyes red-rimmed after a long night spent drinking Grandma Eleanor's wine after they had finished off the bourbon.

Riley tossed the radio at him, harder than she had intended.

"Thanks," he muttered, cocking an eyebrow at her before thumbing the two-way, "Officer Keith Bowman here. Come on down."

The truck's engine rumbled in response, the exhaust stack belching a black cloud of diesel smoke as its big wheels slowly turned towards the farm's dirt road.

"Did you know she called them here?" Riley crossed her arms as she stared at Keith.

"No," his stony gaze was set on the livestock truck as it thrummed down the driveway. "Not until that fucking shouting match upstairs. What time is it?"

She gave him a small snort at the question, waiting for him to remember that none of the clocks worked anymore.

The faintest hint of a grin tugged at his stubbled jaw as he shot her a sidelong glance. Straightening up again, he spread his hands on the veranda's railing, watching as the truck swung around into the yard.

"Hey, how are ya?" a cheery voice called as a man wearing a blue plaid jacket and jeans climbed down from the truck's cabin. He strode towards the veranda's steps with a wide smile and an outstretched hand. "Braxton Shepherd, pleased to meet ya!"

Riley's mouth popped open in surprise.

From his voice over the radio and the looped recording, she had developed a completely different image of Shepherd. Not that she had ever expected to meet him, but she had pictured him as a rugged no-nonsense military man – but he was the polar opposite.

With his graying hair, deep laugh lines and a slightly paunchy physique, Braxton Shepherd looked more like a neighborly handyman who had been in the midst of enjoying an early retirement, well before the end of the world came knocking.

"Keith," Bowman shook Shepherd's hand uncertainly, disarmed by the man's friendliness.

"Riley," she was equally as undecided as she grasped his smooth palm.

"Can't say we have a police officer among us," Braxton folded his arms over the top of his belly, still smiling, "But it sure is great to have ya on board!"

The screen door opened behind them, and Hayden, Greg, Chelsea and Katanya filed out onto the veranda.

In the same instant, a metallic screech pealed across the yard.

Everyone tore their eyes away from Braxton to see the livestock truck's ramp swinging down with a heavy resonating *clang* onto the ground.

A dozen men emerged from the back of the truck, each of them wearing their own combination of fatigues, hunting vests and camouflage jackets.

Seconds dragged as Riley's group stood dumbfounded on the veranda, unable to move as they registered the sudden wave of olive, khaki and brown fanning out across the grass, Shepherd's people brandishing a menacing array of firearms.

CHAPTER 10

"Shit!" Keith Bowman's hand instinctively went towards his hidden shotgun, snatching it up and taking aim over the railing.

Riley rounded on Shepherd as Hayden and Greg stumbled backwards into Katanya and Chelsea, all four of them falling to the floor.

"Hold on, now!" Braxton held up his hands in surrender, staring wide-eyed at Riley's open palm poised to break his nose, "Everybody, calm down. We're all on the same side here. Let's all just take a breath!"

Doing a double take, Riley saw that Shepherd's people had their gun barrels pointed towards the ground, but all the same, they followed his lead, each man raising his trigger hand into the air as a show of peace.

"You should've said something sooner," Keith growled as he lowered his shotgun, although he refused to take his eyes off the dozen armed men. "You know, like maybe give people a fucking warning next time, before you march out the ass-clenching piss-yourself parade."

"We prefer to come armed, just in case," Braxton explained,

sidling away from Riley to offer Greg a helping hand. He shot them all a sheepish smile, "Ya spooked us. Not everyone's as friendly as we hope. We've had a couple bad run-ins these past few weeks. People are getting desperate – even though there's still plenty to go around."

"You got that right," Katanya rose to her feet, helping Chelsea up beside her, "Did you hear about what happened in Clementine?"

"No, I haven't heard from them in a while," Braxton dusted off the back of Hayden's woolen jumper, his eyes suddenly filling with concern, "Are they okay?"

"They're gone," Chelsea tenderly touched the bandage around her head, checking whether the fall had caused yesterday's wound to spring a leak. "All of them."

"That can't be," Braxton clapped a hand to his mouth, looking at each of them in turn.

"People are getting desperate," Greg echoed as he approached the veranda's railing, peering at the livestock truck. "So, when do we leave?"

"That's not the question you should be asking," Riley narrowed her eyes at the blonde Californian beach boy, turning back towards Shepherd. "How many people do you have in your community?"

"More every day," Braxton looked over at his men to see if one of them knew the answer. He shrugged at Riley, "Easily a hundred by now."

"And how do you feed them all?" she asked, pointedly glancing at his belly spilling over his belt.

"Oh, we have a lottery system," he attempted to stifle another smile, poorly though, with his teeth still shining through. "If your number gets called, we eat you!" he broke into a fit of laughter, slapping one of his thighs before waving his hand in the air. "I know, I know – I'm terrible. No, we have hunters, fishers, scavenger teams, and a couple really generous people who were already stocked up on canned goods when the shit hit the fan. Everybody's really dedicated to making this thing work."

"Well, we'd love to help out however we can," Hayden nodded at the others before jerking a thumb over his shoulder. "We've got a vegetable garden out back, bags of pine nuts in the pantry, and a freezer full of game meat."

"Not all of us are going though," Riley reminded him, increasingly aware that she wasn't exactly making the best first impression with Shepherd's people.

"And not all of the food belongs to you," Chelsea chirped out of the side of her mouth.

Riley cocked her head and glared at the blonde college girl.

Katanya had caught most of the meat, Susan had shown them how to harvest the nuts from pinecones, and Grandma Eleanor's vegetable garden had been planted long before any of them had ever even set foot in Nebraska.

She kept her mouth shut though – otherwise she might have pointed out that all of the clothes that Chelsea was wearing right now certainly belonged to Riley.

"Can we stop with all this back and forth bullshit already?" Keith stooped to place his shotgun back on the veranda's wooden floor again, having heard enough. "We've all met the guy now. He's not the hard-ass I thought he was, but he's not a jackass hole-puncher either. I don't think there's any reason not to go. Come on, Riley. Convince your grandma it's the right move while the rest of us load up the truck."

"You heard her last night, she won't –"

"It's okay, Riley," Susan Armstrong opened up the screen door, joining them on the veranda with Aunt Lorraine and Grandma Eleanor shuffling out behind her. "We talked it over upstairs. I don't like the way that it happened either, but Ma said that if she liked him, she'd go."

The small crowd parted, letting the fiery old woman dodder forward for a closer inspection, sizing up Shepherd as he smiled back at her.

"You remind me of my husband," she decided, peering up at him with a shrewd gaze.

"Well, I'm honored," Braxton beamed around at them all with a wide grin, relieved that he had her tick of approval.

"Don't be," Grandma Eleanor's face wrinkled with ridicule. "He was as ugly as sin, with a big stupid smile that only got worse when he got older. And yours looks horrible."

Shepherd's grin faltered as Riley and the others stood on the veranda in stunned silence. Even his men in the yard were glancing at each other uncertainly, when Braxton burst into another fit of laughter, clutching at his sides and wiping his eyes as everyone else joined in, happily cracking up at the man's expense.

"Oh, alright, I'll go," Grandma Eleanor waved her hand dismissively, the shadow of a smirk creasing the corners of her lips. "At least I won't be the oldest person there."

"Don't worry about her," Susan chuckled, shaking her head in embarrassment, "She grows on you."

"I'll bet she does!" Shepherd massaged his cheeks before turning back to his men. "Alright, let's help them with the move. Take what we need, leave what we don't."

Riley's smile faded as she followed the others back inside, certain that she had heard that line before.

CHAPTER 11

Riley Armstrong lingered in the hall by the staircase, watching as her family and friends dispersed throughout the house to pack their things and gather up the supplies.

She wanted to believe that Braxton Shepherd and his group were only there to help, but a small voice inside her head wondered whether the people of Clementine had tricked themselves into believing the exact same thing.

Hearing the makeshift militia's footfalls drum up onto the wooden veranda behind her, she ran up the staircase, taking the steps two and three at a time. Flinging herself around the corner, her sneakers left the landing before the men could open the screen door.

Heart pounding in her ears, she ducked straight into Grandma Eleanor's bedroom, shutting the door softly behind her.

Pupils dilated with her back bracing the entrance, Riley's eyes frantically swiveled around the room.

The curtains were open, but from where she was standing, she could only see the top of the livestock truck idling away in the front yard.

To her left was her grandmother's long dresser, laden with old jewelry boxes and a cumbersome vanity mirror attached.

To her right was the unmade queen-size bed, where she had slept beside Grandma Eleanor last night. And underneath the lamp on the bedside table beside the window was her father's pistol.

Heavy and unfamiliar footsteps sounded on the staircase as Riley bit her bottom lip.

The gun was the obvious choice – but she didn't want to get caught waving around a weapon at Shepherd's people over a fit of her own paranoia.

After all, she hadn't even spared herself a second to think through her thoughts properly. One simple sentence had been enough to set her alarm bells ringing, and yet it had just been a logical phrase coming from a neighborly man.

Just a bunch of paranoid hill folk, her father's words echoed in her mother's voice.

Even so, Riley's heart froze in her chest as someone knocked on the door behind her.

"Hey, anyone inside?" a gruff tone pierced through the wood. "Need a hand with moving anything?"

"Yeah – no – I just…" Riley's voice broke as she looked over her shoulder, as if she could see the man's face on the other side. "Could you give me a few minutes?"

"Sure, take all the time you need," he stepped away from the door, his boots soon fading down the hall.

Riley gulped nervously as she rose out of her brace position, staring intently at the door handle as she backed away from the entrance.

Quickly skirting around the foot of the bed, she lunged for the bedside table and snatched up her father's pistol.

She took a moment to check the safety lever before sliding the gun into the waistband of her jeans at the small of her back, pulling the hem of her gray hoodie down over the handle.

"Just in case," she whispered to herself before gazing out the window at the yard below.

Chelsea was carrying a cardboard box filled with the last of their garden's vegetables.

Hayden, Greg, and a pair of Shepherd's men were struggling with the four corners of the bulky meat freezer, with Aunt Lorraine giving them directions as she trailed along with the power cord.

Keith was standing beside his black crew cab pickup, pointing at the pockmarks peppered across the truck's panels as a thickset man in a hunting vest nodded sympathetically beside him. Riley could almost read the stream of swear words rolling off Keith's lips.

The two men appeared to be supervising a skinny youth as he siphoned fuel from the gas tank into a jerry can. He looked to be about the same age as Riley, but he was practically swimming in the oversized hunting vest that he had clearly borrowed from the man standing behind him.

Katanya emerged from the back of the livestock truck, taking a wide berth of the meat freezer before passing by Susan and Grandma Eleanor, who were standing a few feet away from the veranda.

Riley watched as her mother and grandmother turned to see Braxton Shepherd approaching them, carrying a chair from the dining room. He planted the seat down onto the grass, gesturing for Grandma Eleanor to sit before draping a thick blanket over her shoulders.

As mean as the fiery old woman had been to the warm and

friendly man, she patted his hand in gentle thanks, before turning back towards Susan with a smile.

"What am I doing?" Riley shook her head, crossing the room towards the dresser to pick up a black hair tie.

With her unfounded fears alleviated, she smirked sheepishly at her reflection in the vanity mirror. Brushing her light brown hair back and tying it off into a ponytail, she took one last glance at the serene scene down below before opening the door and heading into the hall.

Hearing a pair of boots approaching from behind, she stood to one side of the corridor, sharing a polite smile with a bearded bald man wearing a camouflage jacket as he passed by with a stack of bed linen.

She watched him descend the staircase and turn the corner, breathing easy as she made her way back towards her mother's bedroom to pack her things.

Riley stopped in the doorway, furrowing her eyebrows.

Her suitcase was lying open on the floor – exactly as she had left it.

But her eyes were magnetically drawn towards the bed frame.

The mattress was gone.

CHAPTER 12

That veil of safety.

That blanket of security.

It was all part of one big rug that had just been pulled out from underneath her.

Riley's ears pricked up as another set of heavy footfalls climbed the staircase.

Icy adrenaline shot through her bloodstream.

Her first instinct was to duck inside her mother's bedroom and go for the window, but through sheer power of will, she held herself rooted to the spot.

She wasn't going to turn tail and run – not while her family and friends were in danger.

Taking three swift steps across the width of the hall, Riley slipped inside Aunt Lorraine's bedroom instead.

Another missing mattress.

At least they had no reason to return to the room.

Leaving the door slightly ajar, Riley rattled the pistol out from the small of her back, listening to the conversation coming up the stairs.

"... think this is the old lady's room," one gruff voice

supposed. "Dunno where the girl went though."

"She'll turn up," a second voice replied as their boots stepped inside Grandma Eleanor's bedroom. "Check the ensuite – might be some good meds."

Gripping her pistol in both hands, Riley flipped off the safety lever and inched across the room to crouch beside the window, making sure to keep the door in her peripheral vision.

A high-pitched screech warbled across the yard.

Greg Preston dropped the box that he was carrying and ran to his sister's side, checking the bandage wrapped around her head.

"THE BEDS! THE BEDS!!" Chelsea screamed hysterically, pointing up at the veranda. "WHY ARE THEY TAKING THE BEDS!?"

A moment later, Shepherd's men hauled the first of the mattresses out into the open.

Aunt Lorraine stood with her arms akimbo, shaking her head at Chelsea and sharing her amused grin with the armed men surrounding them.

Braxton left Susan and Grandma Eleanor with a reassuring smile before turning back towards Chelsea and Greg. He held up his hands in an earnest attempt to calm her down, but his voice was too muffled for Riley to hear anything.

Reaching up to unlock the bedroom window's latches, Riley slid the glass pane open, a wooden groan escaping as the window grated against the old frame.

"Shit, shit, shit," she breathed, ducking back down underneath the sill.

"… don't understand, Chelsea!" Greg yelled over his sister's wails, "They're just mattresses!"

"Think about it for a second," Shepherd's friendly voice

floated up to the second story window, "Where are ya gonna sleep? We need the beds. Just like we need the supplies. But most importantly, we need good people like yourselves to make the magic happen. Ya got nothing to worry about."

"But, in Clementine, the beds…" Chelsea babbled nonsensically, her small voice fading into obscurity.

"That bandage sure looks like ya took a nasty bump to the head," Braxton remarked, hushing her in his warm neighborly tone. "I'll ask Doc Quinn to take a look at it for ya when we get back home."

Riley chanced a glance down at the yard below.

If anyone had heard the sound of the window over the noise coming from Chelsea, their attention was focused elsewhere now.

A chill ran up Riley's spine as she noticed – slowly but surely – Shepherd's men were beginning to reach for their weapons.

Her family and friends were outnumbered and outgunned, and a warning shout would only result in Riley giving away her position.

She hated it, but she knew that if she wanted any chance of making a difference, she had to maintain her silence and wait for the perfect opportunity to present itself.

Katanya locked eyes with Riley from the rear of the livestock truck, when a man's hand shot out and yanked her back inside, pulling her behind the shadows of boxes.

The truck shook for a moment, and then went still.

Catching the flash of movement, Susan bent down to whisper something into her mother's ear.

Keith's stony gaze slid sideways towards the nearest weapon at hand – a hunting rifle, slung over the shoulder of the skinny youth who had siphoned fuel from his gas tank.

"I swear," Aunt Lorraine began, still oblivious to everything happening around her. She thrust a warning finger into Chelsea's bawling face, "If you ruin this for us, I'll –"

"You'll fucking what, bitch!?" Greg rounded on Lorraine. He sized her up, his face twisted with contempt, before shoving her backwards with both hands.

The matronly woman yelped in surprise as she stumbled off balance, toppling over and hitting the ground hard. Rivaling Chelsea's renewed screams, Aunt Lorraine cried out in agony as she gingerly lifted her hips to massage her lower back.

Riley's pulse pounded between her ears.

Seizing advantage of the distraction, she rose up on one knee, rattled a shallow breath, and took aim over the windowsill at the raiders – the wolves dressed in sheep's clothing.

She lined up her sights on one man cradling an automatic. *CRACK!*

Missing her mark, the bullet veered off to the side of his chest, tearing a chunk of flesh from his bicep instead.

The man let out a garbled yell as his fist clenched in a spasm of pain, his middle finger unintentionally squeezing the trigger.

Lead slugs punched holes into the ground, the recoil spinning his mangled arm around, sending bullets flying in every direction.

Chaos and confusion swept across the yard as everybody dove for cover, scrambling for safety from the spiral of death ripping through the air.

Greg grabbed Chelsea and hurled her to the ground, flinging himself down in between his sister and the sudden storm of lead, hugging her from behind, before taking three shots to the back of his rib cage.

From the side of the black crew cab pickup, Keith sprang on top of the skinny youth in the oversized hunting jacket. The adolescent's freckled face gladdened underneath the former policeman's weight, his scrawny frame completely shielded from the spray, but only for a moment.

One split second later, he was choking on his own hunting rifle's shoulder strap as Keith whipped up the weapon and fired round after round at the other raiders. Tangled and staggering, tripping over his own feet, the youth could only cover his ears and yowl for breath with every violent lurch of the gun barrel, instantly coming to the ironic realization that he had become the shield as Shepherd's men began to return fire.

Susan lunged for a bearded bald man's revolver, but Shepherd caught her outstretched hand. Wrapping his arms around her, he lifted Susan up off her feet, carrying her kicking and screaming towards the back of the livestock truck.

Riley took aim, but between her heavy breathing and her mother's limbs flailing, she couldn't pinpoint her gun's barrel on Braxton.

Tough as old leather, Grandma Eleanor threw her blanket over a raider who had thought to use her for cover, blinding him. She clambered to her feet and lifted up her dining chair – her entire body teetering under its weight – before bringing it down on his head, knocking him senseless.

"Hey, shithead!" she dragged the chair after Shepherd with a defiant tone that set her clock twenty years younger, "You take your filthy hands off my daughter, you soft-skinned swine!!"

Braxton turned halfway up the ramp, still holding Susan with one arm as she desperately struggled to wrench free from his grip. There was no trace of his neighborly smile as he eyed the old woman drawing up behind him.

With a heavy sigh, he backhanded Grandma Eleanor across the side of her face, knocking her off the foot of the ramp. He shook his head at the crumpled heap on the ground, feigning remorse, before hauling Susan into the back of the truck.

"Ma!?" Susan yelled, the livestock truck bouncing and rattling as she fought her callous captor, more savage than ever before. "MA!!"

"My glasses!" Aunt Lorraine grasped at the grass, unable to think of anything else amid the gunshots and bellows and Chelsea's screams reaching new heights as the blonde college girl stared, horror-struck, into her brother's lifeless face.

Ducking low behind the windowsill, Riley tore her eyes away from her grandmother's stilled body, spying her next target – the thickset man with the jerry can, sneaking up behind Keith as he downed another raider.

With Hayden missing in action, Keith Bowman was the last ally she could count on.

She couldn't afford to miss her mark this time.

Riley lined up her sights, tracing the big man's beer gut, and pressed the trigger *slow* until it broke.

CRACK!

A flower of blood bloomed from the raider's hip.

He stared down at the fresh wound.

His mouth popped open in disbelief, before his face scrunched up into a ball of rage.

"Fuck," Riley breathed, her fingers trembling as the man closed the distance behind Keith.

She rushed the next shot.

And the next. And the next. And the next.

"Oi, Shepherd!!" Keith thundered over the gunfire as he

rammed his human shield's forehead into the livestock truck's grille, putting the scrawny runt to sleep and freeing up the hunting rifle. "Come out and suck my cuck-making cock, you fucking piece of shit-slurping bitch-turning tits-squirting itch-burning CUN–"

A heavy hollow thud reverberated around the yard, and the rifle fell from his hands.

Keith stood in a trance as the thickset man behind him drew back again, clutching the jerry can in his big meaty hand, preparing to throw all of his weight into the next hit.

Another cold spike of adrenaline shot through Riley's bloodstream, slowing time down to a grinding halt.

Keith's tongue clicked and his stubbled jaw twitched as he gazed up at the big weatherboard home, his empty eyes staring straight through Riley as he searched for the right consonant to finish his sentence.

Pupils dilating, Riley focused on her target again.

She rose up on her knees and leaned out over the windowsill, but she still couldn't get a clear shot.

Her gun's sights were swaying, bouncing from side to side across the thickset raider's shoulders, and Keith's head was square in the middle.

Even from this distance, she could still make out the thin scar just above Keith's eyebrow – a souvenir from the ambush on the freeway, a lifetime ago now.

Images flashed across her mind's eye as she remembered the road to Nebraska – the good times and the bad, like sassing him at a gas station straight after killing three drug addicts in a nightmarish shed – and everything that had happened since.

This was not how it was supposed to end.

But she couldn't risk taking the shot.

She couldn't risk killing the wrong man.

Tears welled in her eyes as she watched the slow-motion arc of the jerry can.

For one fleeting moment, she saw the light spark in Keith's eyes again, his stony gaze refocusing on her.

He mouthed a single word.

A name.

Jesse.

The second hollow drum of the jerry can struck the back of Keith Bowman's head even louder than the first, snapping his jaw shut and sending him to the ground like a felled oak tree.

Riley blinked once.

Twice.

She stared down in disbelief at the broad-shouldered vulgar veteran police officer – the man she had known all her life, the uncle she'd never had, her father's best friend and partner on the force – sprawled face down in the dirt, like he was nothing more than a brain-dead plank of wood.

"YOU MOTHERFUCKER!!" Riley roared, tears streaming down her face as she rained hellfire on the fat sack of shit holding the jerry can, blowing holes through his collarbone, his ankle, his throat, and finally, through his receding hairline straight into his skull.

She shot the ground around him.

She shot the jerry can in his dead hand.

She shot his beer gut until the gun clicked empty, but that didn't stop her from squeezing the trigger, blasting blank baleful bullets at the big bastard's bloody body.

"She's out, boys!" Shepherd shouted in the ear-ringing silence that followed.

CHAPTER 13

"Run, Riley!" Susan Armstrong yelled from the bowels of the livestock truck. "Forget about us! Get outta there!!"

"You've got nowhere else to go!" Braxton Shepherd's voice followed, his six remaining men gathering around him to regroup. "Clementine's gone. There's nothing out there for ya. You'll either starve or freeze to death if ya don't come with us!"

The raiders patiently waited for his signal, the civil snake still set on giving her the illusion of choice.

Riley gripped her empty handgun in bitter resentment, the pistol's slide cocked back at her in grim reproach after her impulsive barrage.

She stared down at Shepherd with the dread of defeat looming over her.

Chelsea's sobs floated up from beside her fallen brother, while Aunt Lorraine sat back against one of the big wheels of the idling livestock truck, breathing hard, gaping wide-eyed at Keith's body.

"This is all your fault," Riley narrowed her eyes at Lorraine. "They're dead because of you, you stupid bitch!"

"There's no need for any of that," Braxton's sickening neighborly tone returned as he helped Lorraine to her feet. He looked back up at Riley, "Now, come on out before we have to come get ya."

"Over my dead body," Grandma Eleanor's voice dripped with venom as she appeared from around the side of the truck's cabin. Her cheek was caved in and her busted dentures were hanging from her lips, but her broken face still held the ferocity of a relentless revenant. She stepped over the thickset bullet-riddled raider's corpse, glowering at Shepherd with the icy blaze of vengeance burning in her eyes. "You call yourselves *men?*"

At a resigned nod from Braxton, the bearded bald raider wearing a camouflage jacket – the same man who had smiled at Riley in the upstairs hall – leveled his revolver at the defiant old woman, and pulled the trigger.

Riley's breath froze in her chest as Grandma Eleanor's head snapped back.

In slow motion, Eleanor Tipton fell to the ground beside the busted jerry can, her taut lips slackening into a glad smile, instantly released from the unimaginable amount of pain that she must have been carrying.

The soft grass of her big weatherboard home's front yard welcomed her into its earthy embrace, as if it had been expecting her for a long time.

"You said you'd bring her with us!" Lorraine hollered at Shepherd, falling to her knees beside her mother's body, her bottom lip trembling. "This… this wasn't what… you said…"

Braxton flinched and turned away as she erupted into wails of anguish, cursing Shepherd and his men and pleading her mother's feeble frame for forgiveness.

This is my home, and I'm going to die here, a faint echo of Grandma Eleanor's voice cooed softly in Riley's ears, as if a gentle breeze had carried her reassuring yet resolved declaration up to the second story window.

Like a final ember of the elderly woman's fiery grit, a glowing cigarette lighter rolled out from her unfurling fingers, setting flame to the spilled contents of the ruptured jerry can.

"Shit!" Shepherd shouted as the yard scorched ablaze. He shielded his face with one arm as he wrenched Lorraine to her feet again, bellowing orders at his men, "Finish loading up what we came for! Back the truck away from the flames! And somebody, get that girl!!"

CHAPTER 14

Angrily rubbing away her tears, Riley Armstrong sprang to her feet as a pair of raiders dashed towards the veranda.

She flung the bedroom door open, barreling across the hall to her mother's room, just as the two men crashed through the screen door down below.

Slamming the door shut behind her, Riley spun towards the wooden tallboy dresser, almost tearing the top drawer off the rails as the sound of heavy boots drummed up the staircase.

Her bleary eyes scanned the empty drawer, as if her missing ammo would suddenly reappear.

Shepherd's men had already taken the spare magazine she had stashed.

"Fuck," she breathed, as the raiders thundered down the hall.

"She's not here!" a shout came from Lorraine's bedroom.

"No shit!" a gruff voice yelled back, "Check the other rooms!"

Icy adrenaline pumping through her veins, Riley threw her empty pistol to the floor and caught hold of the top edge of the dresser, swinging all of her weight towards the door.

The heavy wooden dresser teetered on its bottom corner, but the angle was still too close to the floor, and she couldn't swing gravity over to her side.

Her pupils dilated as the bedroom's door handle spun.

Gritting her teeth, Riley kicked out at the wall, giving her enough leverage to pull the dresser down, the tallboy crashing against the door as it began to open, slamming it shut again just in time.

"She's over here!" the first raider called his companion as he pounded on the timber.

Riley whirled around, bolting across the bedroom towards the window.

She hooked her fingertips underneath the bottom rail and strained, but the window wouldn't budge.

Beads of sweat lined her brow as Shepherd's men rammed their shoulders into the door.

Riley's wide eyes went to the shaking timber, hoping that the dresser would be enough to hold them at bay, when the wooden booms stopped.

"Fuck it, blow the hinges," the gruff-voiced raider decided.

GUVV!!

The door's top hinge exploded into a mess of mangled metal.

Struck by an idea born of desperation, Riley lurched away from the window and dove for her empty pistol on the floor.

GUVV!!

Another finger of hot lead woofed through the door's latch bolt, burying itself into the carpet, half an inch away from Riley's ankle.

She grabbed her handgun by the barrel, her panic-stricken eyes darting towards the top of the door, already leaning into the bedroom.

GUVV!!

Wooden splinters erupted from a fresh hole in the tallboy,

and the pair of raiders punched the door over the dresser.

Scrambling to her feet, Riley rushed back to the window, her knuckles white around the pistol, intent on smashing her way through the glass, when she paused in realization.

The window's latches were still locked.

Cursing herself, she flipped the latches and slid the glass pane open, just as Shepherd's men clumsily clambered over the barricade behind her.

Riley had one leg out the window, when the smaller of the two raiders sprinted across the bedroom and snatched up the scruff of her gray hoodie.

Caught in his grip, she hopped on one foot as he yanked her back inside.

Desperate to escape, Riley lashed out, hammering the hilt of her pistol into the man's face.

His nose splattered, blood spraying out across his cheeks and gushing down his chin.

Her shoulder slammed into the top of the window as the raider let her go, his hands flying up to his face, groaning as he staggered backwards and collapsed over the bed frame, all of his attention focused on trying to staunch the tide of blood, tears and mucus.

Free again, Riley quickly ducked her head underneath the window and climbed out onto the roof, her sneakers squeaking across the slippery tiles.

Lowering herself onto her rump, she prepared to ease herself down to the edge of the roof, when the other man's hand seized hold of her ponytail from behind.

"Gotcha!" the gruff-voiced raider exclaimed, whipping her head back against the wall.

Riley screamed in agony as she felt the roots of her hair rip from her scalp, like fiery needles lancing through her skull.

In her throes, her pistol fell from her grip and slid down out of reach, rattling into the roof's gutter.

She tried to rise to her feet again, but her sneakers scrabbled for purchase on the tiles, with the pain only intensifying as the man wrapped her ponytail around his hand, tightening his hold on her.

"We tried to make it easy on you," the raider grunted from behind as he yanked her hair upwards.

Tears of pain stinging her eyes, Riley reached up to grab at his wrist with both hands.

Using his forearm to lift herself up and ease the pressure on her scalp, she clawed at him with her fingernails, gouging angry red grooves deep into his skin.

His grip didn't falter.

Instead, bristles of coarse hair brushed across her knuckles as the man leaned out over the windowsill, reaching down to wrap his other arm around her midsection.

In the tear-blurred corner of her eye, Riley caught a glimpse of the bearded bald raider in the camouflage jacket as he tried to haul her back in through the window.

"You killed my grandma, you fucking asshole!" she roared, seizing his beard with both hands and dropping all of her bodyweight onto the tiles.

The man's chin smacked the windowsill hard enough to crack the wood, and Riley felt her ponytail sliding out of his loose grip as he slipped into a daze.

She wanted to kill him.

She was well within her rights.

She could have choked him out while his head hung over the windowsill, thrusting her knee into the back of his neck until his face turned blue and his boots stopped kicking.

But glancing through the window, she caught sight of the other raider rolling off the bed frame, his face still a bloody mess as he crawled across the carpet towards his hunting rifle.

Still holding the bald bastard by the beard, Riley lowered her rump onto the tiles again, leaned back, planted her sneakers' heels onto the crown of his skull, and *pushed*.

The raider bellowed in pain as she tore the beard from his neck and chin, snapping him out of his daze as he shot straight up into the air, only to smash the back of his head into the top half of the window.

Riley would have savored the sight, but she was sliding backwards along the tiles, and the edge of the roof was coming up fast.

Throwing the man's freshly-shorn beard to the wind, Riley's hand flailed out for something, *anything*, to grab hold of, but there was nothing.

Her fingertips slipped over the smooth surface of the tiles just as uselessly as the soles of her sneakers.

For one heart-pounding instant, she stared up at the clouds sailing past overhead, the great white shrouds far removed and uncaring about the troubles going on down below, and whether or not Riley Armstrong would break her neck on the ground.

CHAPTER 15

Not today, Riley clenched her fist in defiance as her head went out over the edge of the roof.

She slammed her elbow down on the last row of tiles, anchoring herself for a split second, the momentum of her sliding fall spinning her sideways.

It wasn't enough to stop her from going over, but it gave her just enough time to register the aluminum gutter lining the roof's edge.

Eyes laser-focused, her hands shot out to grab hold of the gutter, curling her fingers around the thin edge of the metal trough as if her life depended on it – because it did.

The aluminum groaned underneath the sudden weight as her lower body slingshotted off the roof, her legs swinging out over the side.

Despite the gutter's sharp edge tearing at her fingers, Riley hung in mid-air with her feet dangling over the back door, grimacing in pain as she stared down at the ground.

She was still high up enough to break her ankle if she botched the landing, and if the raiders were to catch her hobbling away, she might have been better off with breaking her neck instead.

Before she could even visualize herself landing safely though, the gutter groaned again, with its tiny metal supports bending to their absolute limits.

"Fuck," was the only thing that came to her mind as the screws began snapping off, sending her plummeting to the ground.

Her knees absorbed most of the impact, but a surge of pain seared through her groin at the bottom of the jump, doubling her over as the rest of the gutter came crashing down on either side.

Riley struggled upright, fighting through the aching agony in her pelvis as she staggered away, checking herself for blood.

The sharp edge of the gutter had sliced open most of her fingers, but it had also saved her life.

She wasn't out of danger yet though.

The raiders were still on her tail, and the unchecked fire burning in the front yard would soon be blazing out of control.

Doggedly jogging through the pain towards the pine forest in the distance, Riley's heart skipped a beat as she heard the back door swing open behind her.

How the hell did they get downstairs so fast, she glanced back to see the outline of a man sprinting after her.

Riley pumped her aching legs with everything she had, gritting her teeth through the burning throb in her thighs.

She knew that she couldn't outrun him – not like this – but if she could make it past the gravel square and duck into the old farm shed, maybe she could find something to defend herself with.

A moment of regret slipped through her mind as she realized that she had left her father's pistol behind. She was sure that it had fallen into the grass, along with the rest of the gutter, just waiting for her to pick it up again, but it was too late for her to turn back now.

Sucking in lungfuls of air, she was only a few yards away from the barn's dilapidated entrance, when her pursuer's shoes hit the gravel just seconds behind her, closing in quick.

Riley reached out for the shed's door handle, intent on swinging it out wide and bracing herself behind it, using the man's own momentum against him, when his arms wrapped around her waist from behind, sweeping her up off her feet.

With her shoes flailing in the air, she kicked out at the barn's wall, rattling the old shed's dusty bones and sending them both toppling sideways onto the gravel.

Breaking free of her would-be captor's grip as they rolled, Riley rose up on one hand, with her other arm held high, her open palm poised like a soaring eagle, ready to swoop down on its prey, waiting for the very moment he reared his ugly head.

"Riley, what the fuck?" Hayden Marsh gasped as he looked up at her, his pupils dilating at the blood trickling down her predatory palm. "Your fingers, are you okay?"

"It's – it's nothing, I'm fine," she rocked back on her knees to check her fingers again. With all the adrenaline pumping through her veins, she hadn't realized how deep she had sliced her fingers open on the gutter's edge. Her gaze snapped back at Hayden, "Where the hell have you been!?"

"Come on, let's get outta the open," he sprang to his feet, offering her a helping hand as he glanced back over his shoulder.

Riley knocked his hand aside, preferring to clamber back onto her feet on her own. Wounded as she was, this was not the time to show weakness.

They rounded the corner of the shed and sat back against the wall, catching their breath as they listened to the raiders yelling over the livestock truck's revs in the distance.

"That jump – I think you might've strained your groin," Hayden bit the shoulder of his woolen jumper as he ripped the sleeve off. "Two years of college football. Running like that only makes it worse. I was just trying to –"

"You haven't answered my question," Riley couldn't care less if he was an internationally-renowned athlete with a master's degree in exercise physiology. "Where the fuck were you?"

"I was in the wine cellar," he averted his gaze, concentrating on tearing his shorn sleeve to shreds. "Chelsea started screaming, so I dropped the boxes and hid. I heard the gunshots after that, and I knew I made the right choice."

"You fucking coward!" Riley glared back at him in disgust. "You could've made a difference out there! My grandma's dead now. So are Keith and Greg. They've taken my mom, Katanya, Chelsea…" She didn't mention Lorraine. Her aunt had brought this on herself. Riley shoved Hayden, hard, but the big brawny idiot didn't even budge, only making her even madder, "They were your friends! How could you just *hide?*"

"What would you have done?" he snapped back, frowning at her. "If you were me, and you just found out that they were the raiders who killed all the men in Clementine? I saw them carrying out our guns, and all the ammo we had left. What difference would I have made, running out there without a weapon?"

"You could've done *something*," Riley narrowed her eyes at him, unsure of what that something could have been.

"Like what, get shot?" Hayden took hold of one of her hands, wrapping his shredded woolen sleeve around her bleeding fingers, tying it off tighter than necessary.

She resisted the urge to gasp at the pain, but her body betrayed her, one of her heels gouging at the gravel in protest.

He let go of her hand, his hard stare losing its edge.

"Whatever happened to our group…" he sighed, his eyes dropping to the ground, "It's already happened. We can't change it now… But at least I'm still here. And I'm doing *something*."

"Keep telling yourself that," Riley turned away sullenly, even as she offered him her other hand. Flinching at his touch, she toned down her attack, "What made you come outta your hiding spot, anyway?"

"I heard them yelling about a fire," Hayden replied as he wrapped her other hand with the makeshift bandage, gentler this time. "And I didn't wanna get caught in the wine cellar when it got outta control."

"Wine's not flammable, idiot," Riley shot him a look of exasperation before chancing a glance around the corner of the shed.

Flames were already licking up the sides of Grandma Eleanor's big weatherboard home, and the livestock truck's horn was blaring somewhere in the distance, probably already back on the highway by now.

Her eyes fell away from her grandmother's house, blinking back her happy childhood memories as she scoured the yard instead.

There was no sign of her pursuers.

"Come on," she took a deep breath before rising to her feet, starting towards the pine forest. "Let's find Jesse."

Riley froze in her tracks when she laid eyes on Jesse Bowman,

85

already waiting for them at the tree line, on his knees, with a gun to his head.

CHAPTER 16

Riley Armstrong stood side by side with Hayden Marsh, both of them holding up their hands in surrender.

They had no other choice.

The lone gunman from Clementine stared back at them from the tree line, garbed in a green parka and camouflage trousers, blending in with the evergreen pine forest. One of his pistols was on Jesse, while the other traced the space in between Riley and Hayden.

Jesse Bowman's eyes were bloodshot and bleary, as if he had just been kicked awake from his usual haunt – beside his mother's grave.

Having been granted free rein over Grandma Eleanor's wine cellar over the past few months, Jesse's grief had turned to groggy addiction, and his once ropey frame had turned to sallow skin and bones underneath his soiled red shirt.

"Are you with Shepherd?" Riley asked the lone gunman, already knowing the answer. She jerked her head back towards the highway. "Your ride's leaving."

"I could say the same thing," the hooded man replied, his shadowy gaze piercing her. "I'm only gonna ask once – what the fuck have you done with my wife?"

"We don't know who your wife is," Hayden spoke up, glancing sidelong at Riley, as if her story would be any different. "But if you put your guns down, maybe we can help you find her."

"Bullshit," the lone gunman shot at the ground at Hayden's feet, before swinging his barrel up again, plainly stating that his next bullet was bound for blood. "That's how they get you. They pretend they're your friends, and then they kill all the men, and take all the women. The only reason you two are still alive is because you're part of Shepherd's flock."

"You think we're with that asshole?" Riley's throat tightened as old timber crackled and snapped in the distance, her grandmother's big weatherboard home going up in flames behind her. "This is my grandma's farm. We heard Shepherd's broadcast on the radio, and we responded. That's it. We've never met him before today, so you can be damn sure we're not part of anyone's *flock*."

"I saw you in Clementine yesterday," he focused his pistol's sights on Riley, letting her stare down the barrel instead. "After you saw what the raiders did, why'd you let that lady make the call to them last night? It doesn't make any sense – not unless you're working with them."

This guy must have heard Aunt Lorraine on the walkie, Riley exchanged a sidelong glance with Hayden, as if he could read her thoughts. *That's how he knew where to find us.*

"We didn't know the truth about Shepherd until it was too late," Hayden gulped nervously as the gunman eyed them both with suspicion.

Riley's wounded hands wavered in the air.

Her palms would have been damp with sweat if they weren't

already slick with her own blood.

She found herself missing Keith already. The man had never been great at smoothing things over, but he sure had a way with words.

"For fuck's sake!" she yelled, breaking through the tension in her voice as she channeled the vulgar veteran police officer. "You think you're the only victim out here? We've lost people too! My mom just got taken. Wherever your wife is, that's where they're taking our family and friends right now. How about you put your fucking guns down so we can foll–"

"Is that how it works, then?" the man yanked his hood back, revealing himself to be in his late thirties, with a crew cut and dark circles underneath his eyes. He thrust his other pistol's barrel into the base of Jesse's neck. "You pretend to be the last survivors until you can dupe the next people who pick you up. That's what happened here, isn't it? I don't see those two girls you were with yesterday. Stop with all the sob story bullshit. You fucked them over too, didn't you?"

"Just kill them," Jesse croaked in a hoarse voice, "They deserve it. Both of them."

"What the *hell*, Jesse!?" Riley dropped her arms to her sides, glaring at him.

"Keep your hands up!" the gunman barked.

"No, fuck you!" she yelled back, narrowing her eyes at Jesse in disgust. "And fuck you, too! After all the shit we've done for you, while you've done nothing but drink yourself to death out here… and you *want* him to kill us? You're a piece of shit. You know they killed your dad today too, right?"

"He wasn't my dad," Jesse mumbled, his sunken eyes staring down at the shell of an old pinecone, sharing its prickly emptiness. "Stuart was. And you killed him. Right after your mom killed mine… You know what? I'm glad they took Susan. Because now you know what it feels like to lose both of your parents."

"You fucking ungrateful –"

"Riley, don't!" Hayden hugged her from behind, holding her back.

On instinct, she clenched her fists as she struggled in his stubborn sinewy arms, gasping at the jolt of pain searing through her bandaged fingers.

"I'm gonna kill him!" she snarled through clenched teeth, trapped in Hayden's bear hug with her icy glare locked on Jesse.

Remembering her father's self-defense lessons, Riley spread her feet wide apart to keep her balance, before dropping her weight and twisting her torso, freeing up enough room to go to work.

She knew that the easiest way to break Hayden's hold would have been to spin around and knee him in the nuts.

But he wasn't the target – Jesse was.

Riley threw her elbows back at Hayden's muscular midsection, trying to pinpoint his sternum, when a gunshot rang out.

"Enough!" the man in green held one smoking pistol up in the air. He kicked Jesse over, his bony cheek landing on the old pinecone with a crunch. "Sounds like you've got some history, but I didn't see this guy in town yesterday. So maybe you *are* telling the truth."

"Let go of me," Riley twisted again in Hayden's loosening grip.

The moment he broke his bear hug, she turned and aimed a don't-ever-do-that-again kick at his shin with the toe of her sneaker, reigniting the fiery ache of her strained groin while Hayden groaned and hopped around on one foot.

"The three of you are gonna help me get my wife back," the gunman decided, holstering his weapons.

"And what makes you think we're gonna do that?" Jesse rose up on his hands and knees, brushing broken pinecone scales from his face.

"Because he's gonna help us get my mom back," Riley pressed her thumbs into her throbbing thighs as she stared sidelong at Hayden, "And you owe it to your friends."

She had no idea what to expect from a stranger, who had conveniently happened to show up just minutes after they had been attacked, but without any weapons or transport of their own, they didn't really have a choice. Not if they wanted a chance at saving what was left of their group.

"Let me rephrase," Jesse staggered to his feet, his soiled red shirt hanging from his scraggy frame. He wiped his hands on his jeans, "What makes you think *I'm* gonna do that?"

"Who cares what *you* do?" Riley cocked her head at him in disdain, "You wanted us dead a minute ago. We're better off without you."

He stared back at her indifferently, his empty bloodshot eyes neither happy nor hurt at the thought of being alone.

"Take a good look around, Jesse," Hayden gingerly eased his weight back onto his injured leg as he gestured towards Grandma Eleanor's blazing home behind them. "You're not getting your next buzz here. What are you gonna do when the withdrawals kick in?" he raised his eyebrows at Jesse, waiting for an answer that never came, before shrugging at Riley, "He might be good for something."

"Yeah, fucking meat shield," she snorted with contempt,

looking back towards the man in the green parka. "Okay, Camo Pants, where's your vehicle? We need to follow that truck before they disappear."

"No need," the gunman turned back towards the pine forest, "We already know where they're going."

"Who's we?" Riley's question hung in the air as they watched him disappear into the trees.

CHAPTER 17

"Hey, Camo Pants!" Riley yelled ahead as they limped after the lone gunman's long strides. "Wait for us!"

Her groin was still aching from the botched jump, and both Hayden's shin and Jesse's hangover were slowing them down. All three of them were lagging behind as they hiked along the game trail twisting in between the towering evergreen pine trees.

"Name's Sterling Granger," the man in green called over his shoulder. "And you're gonna have to keep up – we need to get clear of this forest before the wind changes direction."

Riley glanced back at the other two as they stumbled through the ferns growing over the path. Through the foliage behind them, she could see black smoke rising up over the treetops, blowing back towards the highway.

"How long do we have to walk?" she winced as she picked up the pace.

Despite how many times she had gone camping with her parents as a child, as well as foraging for fallen pinecones over the past few months, she had no idea just how far the forest stretched.

"There's an old highway just on the other side of these mountains," Sterling replied casually, as if the nearest ridge wasn't at least an hour's trek away. "We've got the daylight on our side though, so it'll be faster than it took to get here."

"Were you walking all night?" Riley panted through the pain in her pelvis.

"Soon as we heard the chatter over the radio," he stopped at a fork in the path, looking up at the ridge in the distance before turning left. "Didn't wanna risk taking the highway, but I figured you'd be close enough to reach on foot."

"How did you know it was us?" Riley paused to glance back at Hayden and Jesse, making sure that they knew which way to turn before following Granger again.

"I didn't," Sterling shrugged without looking over his shoulder. "I was just hoping to save some innocent people from falling into the same trap we fell into. I need a few more hands if we're gonna take on Shepherd."

"I thought you already had people of your own?" Riley asked as she stepped around a small pile of animal droppings on the trail.

"Not enough," he replied, scanning through the trees to look at the smoke again. "Not nearly enough."

"Do you know how many men Shepherd has?" she puffed behind him, the game trail's gentle slope giving way to an incline.

"Can't say for sure," Granger answered, not breaking his stride as he glanced back at her. "But you saw Clementine. You can bet he rolled up with a lot more than one truck when they took that town."

"How many towns have they taken?" Riley wondered as she stared down at her sneakers, focusing on putting one foot in front of the other, trying to shut out the pain in her thighs by losing herself to the conversation.

"Most of them have just been small settlements," Sterling replied as the trail curved to the right. "Campgrounds, caravan parks, farms like your grandma's. First major one I saw was yesterday, in Clementine, but we figure he must've taken Burview a while back, otherwise he wouldn't have that radio tower broadcasting his bait message."

"My stupid fucking bitch of an aunt…" Riley seethed, her anguish turning into anger. "I swear, if I ever see her again, I'm gonna leave her dumb ass behind with Shepherd's rotting corpse."

"*When* you see her again," he corrected, still holding onto the hope that getting their loved ones back wasn't just a pipe dream. "And you should be grateful that you'll still have someone to blame when this is all over. We fell for the same damn bait message back at the ranch. It was my brother who made the call… I buried him a couple weeks ago."

"I'm sorry," she looked up to see Granger pull the hood of his parka up over his head. "What happened?"

"Same shit that happens to everyone else, I guess," Sterling supposed, his strides growing longer. "Make the call. Chat back and forth for a while. See whose setup sounds better. Realize how fucked you are for the winter. Agree to get picked up in the morning… You know the rest."

"How did you survive?" Riley wondered whether he had hidden, like Hayden in the wine cellar, or if he had fought back.

After narrowly avoiding Sterling's rain of bullets in Clementine, she could scarcely imagine how hard-pressed the raiders would have been to take his wife and kill his brother.

95

"I wasn't there," Granger lowered his head. "I was... being fucking stupid. I was stashing supplies somewhere nobody would think to look. You know, just in case Shepherd's place didn't come as advertised. Not a lot, but enough to get by if we needed it in a pinch. Food, water, Abbie's – my wife's – meds. Ammo, a couple weapons. All that good shit. But then –"

His breath hitched, and he stopped in his tracks.

Riley almost walked into the back of him, teetering on her toes.

"Then my truck wouldn't start again," Granger leaned one hand against a tree trunk with a sigh, "Can't call anyone for a tow these days. I had to run the rest of the way back to the ranch just so I wouldn't miss our ride. I was calling my wife's name – I knew she wouldn't leave without me. I ran up that driveway like I had a damn dog snapping at my heels. And then I saw it."

He sniffed before resuming his long strides up the slope again, compelling Riley to follow.

"Fucking bloodbath..." he continued, his vengeful grief driving every step forward, "My brother. Our ranch hands. Couple survivors we picked up in Clementine... All dead. Abbie gone. Women gone. They even took the fucking shovels." He rubbed at the dark circles underneath his eyes, pulling himself from the depths of his memory. "I've gotta get her back. My Abbie, she's a strong woman, but even she can't survive for too long without her meds. And those fucking animals – they're just gonna use her until she's gone."

A long stretch of silence fell between them.

Riley didn't know what to say.

Yesterday, the lone gunman garbed in green was a bogeyman

hell-bent on blasting bullets into her back. And now, he was spilling his struggles while they hiked up the mountain, both survivors of the same foe.

She had barely even allowed herself enough time to process the events of that morning. And yet somehow, it was far easier to feel sympathy for a stranger than deal with her own trauma.

They broke through the trees into a clearing, and Riley was surprised to see that they had already reached the ridge.

She turned around in a slow circle, gazing at the picturesque scenery sprawled out down below.

The midday sun had already burned through the stubborn chill of the autumn air, bathing the rural landscape in its golden warmth. Boughs of yellow and orange leaves speckled the green of the forest, the impostor trees among the evergreen pines unable to keep up their act any longer. Vast fields of grass swayed in the wind, with private reservoirs shimmering on the paddocks in the distance.

For one blissful moment, Riley felt an overwhelming urge to whip out her phone and snap a photo.

She wouldn't post it online for anyone else to see.

Not that she could, anyway.

But she wanted to hold onto this moment forever.

And then she remembered.

She had left her dead phone in her suitcase, along with the rest of the rare glimpses of happiness that she had managed to capture before her battery had died.

Whatever moment she had wanted to hold onto slipped away as Hayden and Jesse emerged into the clearing behind them. Jesse's arm was slung across Hayden's shoulders, the former college footballer apparently having gotten over the kick to his shin.

"Finally," Jesse slumped down onto the ground, "It's about time we took a break. My head's killing me."

"I can keep going," Hayden bragged, before a shadow of self-doubt crossed his face as he looked around at the rest of them. "Did anyone bring any water?"

"Yeah, I've got a gallon in my backpack," Riley sassed him with half a smirk. "Didn't you see me lugging it up the mountain?"

Slow to catch on, he searched the clearing for her non-existent backpack.

"No time for breaks," Granger declared grimly from his perch atop a nearby boulder. "Wind's turning."

Riley followed his shadowy gaze down to the black plume of smoke rising up from Grandma Eleanor's farm.

The thick haze was beginning to bend back towards the pine forest.

"Let's move!" Sterling barked at Jesse. He turned to Riley and Hayden, still on their feet. "We need to double-time it down the mountain, before that blaze turns into a full-blown bushfire!"

CHAPTER 18

"Shit!" Riley Armstrong flailed out over the ledge as she charged into a sudden drop, her shoes still running in mid-air.

Her bloodied and soiled hands caught hold of an overhanging tree branch as she fell, barely managing to swing herself backwards before the thin limb snapped under her weight.

She landed on her back against the steep dirt slope and slid the rest of the way down, rolling and crumpling into a heap at the bottom.

Dust clouds flew up from the rugged trail, criss-crossed with old mountain bike tire tracks. This wasn't the way she would have chosen out of the forest – especially given her current condition – but they didn't have any other choice.

Their two options had been to either bleed and maybe break a few bones on the way down, or take the slow route, choke on smoke and fall to a crawl until the bushfire caught up to burn them alive.

Riley lurched to her feet again, heart hammering in her throat and aching agony blazing through her thighs.

The makeshift bandages around her throbbing fingers were already coming apart, but she had no time to stop and fix them, a thin veil of smog hovering above the pine forest.

Pushing herself through the pain of her strained groin, Riley skipped and skidded down the next dip in the track, mere moments before Jesse came crashing down on her heels, calling for help.

"Keep moving, dickhead!" she yelled over her shoulder.

Hayden and Sterling were leading the way, sliding down slopes and leaping over logs, like the mountain bike trail was nothing but an obstacle course for them. And by the way they were keeping pace with each other, Riley could tell that they were in the heat of an undeclared race.

Every sharp twist and steep fall brought her body a little closer to the brink of breaking, but no matter what the track's rough terrain threw at her, she forced herself to keep going.

Whatever she had to endure, she knew that the pain would pale in comparison to the suffering that her mother was going through. Riley could only imagine the horrible things that Shepherd's men had in store for the captured women.

The momentum of the turbulent downward trail catapulted her across a sharp turn, sending her reeling sideways into a fallen tree. But even as she felt the coppery taste of blood in her mouth, it was the thought of Braxton Shepherd that made her grimace.

With every tree trunk that she slammed her shoulders into, every offshoot branch that clawed at her torso, every rock that she stumbled over – she could see the civil snake's sickening neighborly smile, the man's deep laugh lines creasing as he watched them run.

It was as if Shepherd was in the forest with them, tormenting her.

He had arrayed his inanimate raiders all over the mountainside, with every tree trunk another bastard's body to bowl over, every offshoot branch another limb to snap, and every rock another skull to stomp.

If the broken bike trail was an obstacle course for Hayden and Sterling, then for Riley, it would be her crucible.

Every drop, twist and crash setting her body ablaze was all designed to beat the weakness out of her.

She was going to emerge victorious at the bottom of the mountain with nothing but strength remaining – like a phoenix reborn from the ashes.

At least that was the mantra her mind was clinging to.

Any fanciful idea was better than accepting the truth.

Riley Armstrong was a human pinball.

Her legs were heavy and lumbering, numbly carrying her from one collision to the next. Her hands were caked with blood and dirt, too weak to slow her descent as she rag-dolled down every set of giant stairs. And all the while, her brain rattled around in her skull with every impact, dazed and detached, just another punch-drunk passenger along for the ride.

By the time she reached the bottom of the mountain, she didn't know whose screams were filling her ears.

CHAPTER 19

"Let me go," Riley Armstrong murmured as she stirred awake, her head lolling on her chest, staring down at the sheet of asphalt drifting past underfoot.

"No fucking way," Hayden panted beside her.

She was suspended in between Hayden Marsh and Sterling Granger, her numb arms draped over their shoulders as her sneakers dragged across the surface of the road.

"I can walk," she insisted, barely able to lift one foot off the ground.

She didn't want to give either of them any reason to believe that she was a liability.

"Swallow your pride," Granger grunted from the other side, "We're almost there."

Riley raised her head just enough to see that they were still in the middle of the forest.

Aspen, birch and hickory trees marched past on either side of the highway, wearing scanty robes of bright yellow, pale gold and burnt orange.

They were nearing a T-intersection up ahead, with an old weather-beaten truck stop tucked away on the left. One lonesome brick building dominated the desolate concrete lot, its rusty tin roof huddling over a pair of gas pumps like they were its most prized possessions.

Even before the apocalypse had brought the entire country grinding to a standstill, Riley doubted that the secluded truck stop had ever seen enough traffic to turn a profit. By the size of the weeds that were growing through the cracks in the concrete, this place had been abandoned a long time ago.

"Where are all of your people?" Riley turned her head to stare sidelong at Sterling.

"You're about to meet him," he slowed their pace to a halt just outside the concrete lot, easing her arm from around his shoulders.

"That's far enough!" a baritone voice boomed out from the brick building, a rifle's barrel emerging from a crack in one of the grime-streaked windows.

"Relax, Virge," Sterling held up his hands as he walked across the gravel shoulder. "It's just me, and I've brought some friends."

"You vouch for 'em?" the rifle didn't waver.

"Yeah, this is the group from last night," he replied, lowering his arms. "I didn't get there in time. Shepherd's flock took the rest."

"I know, I heard," the rifle withdrew from the window.

Granger glanced back over his shoulder, giving them the okay to approach.

"Warm welcome," Riley let out a pained snort as she took an agonizing step forward.

"Best welcome anyone can hope for these days," Hayden supposed, half-carrying, half-dragging her behind Granger towards the entrance.

"Where's Jesse?" she would have looked around, but all of her concentration was focused on trying to support her own weight as they walked.

"Didn't think you cared," Jesse's scraggy frame trudged into view beside them, both of his hands stuffed into his pockets.

There were scratches all over his face, neck and arms, with patches of his soiled red shirt torn open, hanging in strips, revealing his pale scrawny shape underneath. Along with his sunken eyes, he looked about as good as Riley felt.

"I don't," she fired back as they passed underneath the shade of the rusty tin roof. "Keith did though. Your name was the last thing he said before they killed him."

"That was nice of him," Jesse shrugged before sauntering inside after Sterling.

"Fucking asshole," Riley stared at the back of his head in disbelief.

"Kid's got daddy issues," Hayden agreed with half a smile. "But he called us back when he found you face down at the bottom of the trail. Told you he'd be good for something."

She silenced him with a glare.

It was going to take a lot more than asking others to carry her before she would forgive Jesse for how much of a selfish prick he'd been over the past few months. And that was before he had celebrated her mother's kidnapping.

The inside of Virge's truck stop was almost as bare as the desolate concrete lot.

The sparse shelves were down to packets of chips and chocolate bars. The refrigerators were still working – there was no lack of fuel for a generator in a gas station – but there were only a few sodas and energy drinks left in the fridge cases.

An old wooden desk stood in one corner, housing a crackling CB radio beside a half-empty bottle of whiskey.

Naturally, Jesse made a beeline for the desk.

"Can we get a first aid kit over here?" Hayden sat Riley down on the front counter and strode towards the row of fridges at the back of the store, in a vain search for bottles of water.

"Nice to meet you too," the proprietor zoomed out from behind a shelf, snatching the bottle of whiskey out of Jesse's hand before he could unscrew the cap. "Help yourselves, why don't you?"

Eyeing them all with a scrutinizing squint, Virge took a long pull from the bottle. Curls of gray hair sprouted from underneath the brow of his black beanie as he leaned back, the liquor fueling his ruddy complexion.

He breathed out the burn with a discontented scowl. A set of dog tags jingled over his army fatigues as he screwed the whiskey's lid back on, dropping the bottle beside the rifle cradled across his lap.

"Virge Norton," Sterling made the introduction as he marched around the counter, digging up a first aid kit and blowing the dust off, "Meet Riley, Hayden and Jesse."

"Fuck away from my desk, Jesse," Virge grumbled from his wheelchair.

"Hear anything on the airwaves?" Sterling asked as he unboxed a bottle of antiseptic and beckoned Riley's bloody fingers closer.

"Just the usual post-mission bullshit," the old man replied, biting the lid off a red marker and adding another cross to a map on the wall, "Heard they put up a good fight."

Riley gritted her teeth as the antiseptic stung through her open wounds, igniting the cuts on her fingers with a burning sensation.

"Why didn't you warn us?" she looked over at the crackling CB radio before giving them both an accusing glare. "You've got a microphone here. You could've told us last night after we made contact with Shepherd, and we would've had plenty of time to prepare."

"We couldn't take the risk," Virge frowned back at her. "If they knew we were listening, they'd start looking for us. They could try to lure us out with false information. Or maybe they could start targeting all the truck stops in the area – anywhere with a CB. And you know what happens to the men they find."

"A warning wouldn't have made a difference anyway," Hayden came back to the front counter with a handful of energy drinks, tossing a can over to Jesse. "It's not like Lorraine would've told the rest of us."

"That's not the point," Riley winced as Sterling wrapped a bandage around one of her hands. She redirected her pain towards the old man. "How many other places have fallen because you were too much of a pussy to get on the radio? How many bloodbaths could you have prevented? My mom, my grandma… all of our friends are either dead or taken, all because you were too chickenshit to talk into a fucking mike!"

Hayden looked back and forth between Riley and Virge, shifting his weight uneasily.

Sterling focused on wrapping her fingers, choosing not to say anything.

Jesse cracked open his energy drink and slurped loudly in the silence.

"Well, you can get the fuck outta my shop," Virge raised his eyebrows, staring at the three newcomers in turn. "Granger, make sure they don't steal anything on their way out. I'd hate to waste a bullet."

"We're all leaving," Sterling put a pin through Riley's bandage and started working on her other hand, "Soon as this is done. There's a bushfire headed our way. Gonna need you to pull your car out front. We'll load up whatever we can carry."

Take what we need, leave what we don't, Riley almost echoed Braxton Shepherd's words, but the thought made her shiver.

"Fuck off, you're not serious," Virge studied Sterling's grim expression for a moment before spinning his wheelchair and disappearing behind a shelf. A mothballed curtain moved to one side, followed by a muttered curse as the old man rolled towards a door in the back.

"What was the point of chewing him out like that?" Hayden asked Riley as he reached over the counter for a stack of plastic bags. Shaking one open, he began clearing out what little sustenance was left on the shelves, "We're all on the same side here, aren't we?"

"Yeah, until push comes to shove," she answered bitterly, reflecting on the individual actions that had led them into this mess. "Chelsea and Greg couldn't handle the thought of wintering at the farm. Lorraine couldn't see past herself when she invited the raiders right to our doorstep. Even you hid in the wine cellar until the fire broke out. I'm so sick of everyone putting themselves first, and not caring about the consequences for anyone else."

Hayden drew a breath as if he was about to say something that would justify his act of cowardice, but his shoulders dropped instead, his eyes turning downcast before moving on to the next aisle.

"That's what happens when you trust other people," Jesse took another slurp of his energy drink before tossing the half-empty can across the store. Loping towards Virge's desk in the corner, he began rifling through the drawers. "You fool yourself into thinking they've got your best interests at heart... and then they kill your parents."

"Jesse, I told you what hap–"

"You were right," Sterling cut across Riley as he put a pin through her second bandage, "About what you said to Virge. If he could've warned my brother about Shepherd a couple weeks ago, but chose not to, I'd be just as pissed. Truth is though – none of us knew what we were up against back then."

Riley opened her mouth to remind Sterling that he could have warned them over the microphone, just as easily as Virge, but she bit back her tongue.

She had already picked enough fights with the few remaining allies she had left.

"But now we do," Sterling continued, sidling past Jesse towards the map on the wall. He pointed at a red circle marked on the chart. "This is Burview, where they've got that radio tower broadcasting Shepherd's bait message." His finger traced southwest to another red circle, "And here's Lake Springworth, this is where –"

"Lake Springworth?" Riley echoed, furrowing her eyebrows in faint recognition. "I remember back when I was a kid, my parents would talk about that place every now and then, but never in a good way."

"Couple people claimed it was some kinda cult community," Sterling replied, his lips twisting skeptically as he narrowed his eyes at the lake. "My brother used to say that anyone who went there either got lost or never came back home the same... But my brother was full of shit," he snorted, recalling the rumors.

He concluded with a shrug, "Doesn't make a difference what it was – we're ninety percent sure this is where Shepherd's keeping all the women they've kidnapped."

"And is that the other ten percent?" Jesse nodded at a red question mark on the map as he fished a full bottle of whiskey out of the desk's bottom drawer.

"No," Sterling frowned at the chart before turning back to Riley. "They've got a poultry farm supplying them from somewhere down in Long Plains, we just don't know where yet. But this is the reason why we had to stay off the air – so that we could listen in for long enough to know how to hit them where it hurts."

"I don't give a shit where they're keeping their chickens," Riley staggered to her feet, lurching over to a nearby shelf to hold herself upright. "I just want my mom back. How far is that lake from here?"

"There's no way we're getting near that lake without getting shot to shit," he warned, tapping a single road on the map leading to the body of water, flanked by forests on both sides. "We need to draw away their strength before we can even think about mounting an assault."

"What about the radio tower?" Hayden asked, dropping a bag full of junk food on the counter. "At least we'll be able to stop that looped recording. Maybe save some other survivors from giving away their positions."

"We thought about that," Sterling glanced at the crackling CB radio, "But from the sound of his bait message, Shepherd's got Burview under heavy guard as well. That poultry farm is the last piece of the puzzle. We can sabotage it and wait for them to –"

"Play right into an ambush," Riley finished, using her

bandaged hands as leverage along the rows of empty shelves, studying the map as she inched forward past the aisles.

Somewhere outside, an engine roared, followed by screeching tires.

Hayden ducked behind the front counter.

Sterling tore the map off the wall.

Jesse cracked open the whiskey and took a few hearty gulps.

Too sore to spring into action, Riley faltered her way around the last shelf, keeping a wary eye on the pair of gas pumps outside.

She reached for the waistband of her jeans at the small of her back, clumsily clutching at nothing as she bitterly remembered that her father's pistol was gone.

A burly red minivan pulled up beside the store's entrance, with Virge behind the wheel.

He blared the horn, eyes blazing at the sight of Jesse drinking his whiskey.

"That's our ride outta here," Sterling rolled up the map and started towards the door. "Let's move."

Hayden sheepishly rose up from behind the counter, brushing his shoulders off before packing up the first aid kit.

"Riley, you need a hand?" Sterling asked as he swung the door open.

"No, I'm gonna hang back for a minute," she replied, lurching towards the desk to pore over the CB radio. "Is this on channel four?"

"It's a bit late to start warning people," Jesse leaned against the wall, eyeing her with amusement as she tried to make sense of the dials.

"Come on, Riley," Hayden urged as he hauled the supplies outside. "We don't have time for this. The flames are gonna cut us off if we stay any longer!"

"That's why I'm gonna lure Shepherd's men here," she glanced back over her shoulder at him. "We need to bleed their strength. Nobody's gonna suspect foul play if they die in the fire."

"Good thinking," Sterling crossed the room to examine the radio. "Looks like Virge was monitoring their private channel." He spun the dials, tuning the frequency through waves of static to the designated helpline. "Alright, ready to go. Don't oversell it."

"Have fun with that," Jesse screwed the cap back on his stolen whiskey, his pale face flushing with a crude grin. "I'll be in the car with our hide-and-seek champion and semi-sober Santa. Try not to get yourselves left behind."

Ignoring him, Riley thumbed the microphone's button, fighting the urge to shower Shepherd with a string of curses.

"Hello?" she asked in a warped voice, "Is anyone there?"

No response.

"Give it a minute," Sterling stared at the radio intently.

"We don't have a minute," Riley whispered back, as if they could hear her with her thumb off the button.

Virge blared the horn again, jabbing his finger at them through the passenger window and gesturing for them to *get in the fucking car, you stupid motherfuckers*. He turned in his seat and began growling at Hayden and Jesse in the back.

"Hello?" Riley thumbed the microphone again, "Is this the line for Mr Shepherd?"

Hayden lumbered out of the minivan to burst through the door.

"Hurry up!" he shouted, one foot in the store, the other turned back towards the idling vehicle. "Virge is gonna leave without you!"

"Fuck it," Sterling held up a hand, pleading for patience from Virge. "Sell it."

"Please, if anyone's out there," Riley put on her best damsel-in-distress voice, "It's just me and my two sisters. We're outta gas and we're stuck at a truck stop in the middle of a forest. There's a big fire coming down the mountain, I don't think we can outrun it. Please..."

No response.

"That's it, we need to move," Sterling seized her arm and hooked it around his shoulders, hauling her away from the desk.

Hayden was already back inside the burly red minivan.

Virge shook his head behind the wheel, muttering curses under his breath before launching an unsuccessful lunge at the bottle of whiskey in Jesse's hand.

Riley stared back at the CB radio as Sterling kicked the door open.

"Found ya," Shepherd's voice crackled through the radio. "We're on our way."

CHAPTER 20

"May as well deepthroat my rifle and say good night!" Virge Norton fumed from behind the wheel of his burly red minivan, his collapsed wheelchair and rifle stowed in a compartment beside the center console.

They were idling on a back road, barely visible from the highway, but still in view of the truck stop sitting on top of the T-intersection.

The bushfire was sawing its way down the mountain now, its jagged edge lined with a hellish hue.

A family of elk stampeded across the highway, some of them tripping over their own hooves on the asphalt, their eyes filled with panic as they fled the flaming forest.

"The plan's not that bad, Virge," Sterling spoke up from the backseat as the animals disappeared into the woods on the other side of the road. "We wait for the raiders to come through, pop a couple rounds and then take off."

"Oh, well, why didn't you say so?" Virge glared up at the rearview mirror, "You fucking ass-monkey. Do you have any idea how to read a map? We turn left and it's Long Plains. We turn right and it's Lake Springworth."

"Good thing there's a third option," Jesse supposed, sitting in between Hayden and Sterling in the backseat. He nodded towards the highway heading east at the bottom of the T-intersection.

"Who let this clown outta the fucking circus?" the grizzled war veteran made the effort to turn around in his seat this time, his dog tags jingling. "If there's one sane bastard in Shepherd's flock, they'll be coming down *this* fucking road!"

"Then we're back to going either left or right," Hayden concluded with a shrug. "At least we probably won't run into anyone on the way."

"That simple, huh?" Virge redirected his glare, "Okay, let's say I'm stupid enough to drive down a highway next to a fucking forest fire – which way should we turn, genius? Left or right? Or should we flip a fucking coin?"

"We don't need to guess," Riley murmured from the front passenger seat. "We wait until Shepherd's people come through, kill them all, and then hightail it outta here."

"Sure, *you* can wait for Shepherd," Virge raised his eyebrows at her. "There's a spot over there on my porch, just for you. And while you're sitting there waiting, you can go fuck yourself!"

"Sounds like a good plan," Jesse piped up from the backseat. "But Riley couldn't shoot a target to save her life. Not unless she was holding a gun at point blank range and they were all lined up on their knees, unarmed, begging for mercy."

Riley gave him a small snort as she remembered the flash of fear in Stuart Sinclair's eyes, the pathetic pleas of Jesse's cowardly stepfather forever etched in her memory, right before she blew the self-serving son of a bitch's brains out all over Grandma Eleanor's wooden veranda.

114

"What if we just hide here until they drive past?" Hayden suggested, ripping Riley from her remorseless reminiscence as they watched the bushfire blaze down the mountain. "Then we speed off and hope the flames take care of them."

"That's not gonna work," Sterling shook his head as he looked out the window. "Wouldn't take long for them to check the truck stop, realize there aren't three women waiting for a rescue after all, and then turn back around. I mean, even if we had a head start… Virge, how fast does this thing go?"

"Not fast enough," the old man replied, reaching across the center console to pull a black walkie from the glove box. He sighed in resignation, "May as well find out how much longer I have to put up with this pinhead parade."

He thumbed the two-way's power button, the small display screen flashing to life. The frequency was already set to channel four, with a healthy battery gauge in the upper corner.

"… Ma'am, if you're still there," a raider's voice crackled over the radio, "Our ETA is two minutes."

"Maybe we should cover the car with leaves," Hayden sat up suddenly, looking around at the trees surrounding the back road that they were idling on.

"You wanna rake up a pile of autumn leaves?" Virge squinted up at the rearview mirror.

"They'll see the movement," Sterling cautioned, staring down the highway. "Our best chance for going unnoticed is if we all stay in the van. Maybe when they pass by, they'll think this is just another abandoned vehicle that ran outta gas. We need the element of surprise on our side if we're gonna get outta here alive."

Riley watched through her window as clouds of black smoke billowed high above the flaming forest, sparks and cinders flying with every falling tree, the raging inferno forging on towards them in its inexorable appetite for destruction.

Back in the pre-apocalyptic world, all manner of fire fighting resources would have been dispatched to drown the flames, desperate to bring the blaze back under control before it got out of hand.

But without the emergency services on call, or any of the old infrastructure that they had all relied on for so long, Riley could only imagine just how widespread Grandma Eleanor's wildfire would become.

"Here we go," Sterling whispered as a mud-bellied pickup truck crested a rise on the highway in the distance.

He dropped out of sight, along with Hayden, pulling Jesse down in between them.

Riley ducked below the dashboard, her strained groin grating in agony as her legs bunched up underneath the glove box.

The pickup truck's engine rumbled into earshot, contending with the roar of the flames.

Virge hunched over the steering wheel, his wary gaze tracking the raiders through the trees.

He breathed a sigh of relief as they hurtled past, their tires screeching to a halt just outside the truck stop.

Riley eased herself back up into the passenger seat, peering through her window as four men jumped out of the mud-bellied pickup truck, two of them carrying automatics.

In the corner of her eye, she caught a glimpse of orange in her side mirror.

At first, she disregarded it as a dull glimmer of autumn leaves rippling in the wind, but doing a double take, her heart leapt up into her throat.

"It's behind us," she bit her bottom lip, glancing sidelong at Virge.

"Fuck," he breathed, looking up at the rearview mirror in alarm.

"We've gotta move," Riley whipped her head around to stare through the rear window, "Right now."

While all of their focus had been on the truck stop and the bushfire blazing in the distance behind it, they hadn't realized that the flames had already swept down the mountain and across the highway, closing in on them from the rear.

"Nobody's home," the radio crackled as Shepherd's men delivered an update.

"Sweep the area," Braxton's voice came back. "Ma'am, we're gonna need ya to come on out."

"They'll see us for sure if we make a move now," Hayden gulped nervously in the backseat, glancing over at the four men scouring the truck stop's desolate concrete lot.

"No choice," Sterling drew the pair of pistols holstered on his waist as he locked eyes with Virge. "How do you wanna die?"

"Drunk and quick," Jesse answered, taking another swig of his stolen whiskey.

"May as well go out guns blazing," the grizzled war veteran shrugged, turning on the engine's ignition.

He flicked a switch, and a flood of acrid smoke rushed into the minivan as the front passenger window cracked open.

Riley erupted into a fit of hacking coughs as Sterling wound his window down in turn.

"That smell sure takes me back," Virge grinned, lifting his rifle over Riley's lap to lay the barrel's tip on the half-open glass. His gaze slid sideways as she masked her face with the front of her hoodie, "Might wanna cover your ears while you're at it."

"Wait!" she yelled, glancing back at Sterling before he could climb out the window, both men frowning back at her, "Aim for their tires, and they won't be able to chase us."

"Fuck it," Virge shrugged, squinting down the length of his barrel, "Let 'em burn."

GUVV!!

The blast was deafening in the confines of the minivan, the force of the gunshot making the passenger window crack.

Shouts of alarm went up in the truck stop as Shepherd's men ducked for cover.

"Bullseye, bitch," Virge muttered as he cocked another round into the chamber, resting the rifle's barrel on the cracked glass again as he took aim at the pickup's second back tire.

GUVV!!

The passenger window shattered this time, showering Riley with an explosion of glass crystals as Virge shoved his rifle back into its compartment beside the center console.

"We're taking fire!" one of Shepherd's men roared into the radio.

His eyes alive with the thrill of the kill, Virge slammed the minivan into gear and punched the accelerator, gunning the engine out onto the highway, fishtailing across the asphalt as their wheels spun for traction.

Hayden and Sterling dropped down in the backseat as a barrage of hot lead hammered into the rear.

Jesse simply took another pull of whiskey, unfazed, even as a salvo of slugs sprayed through the back window.

The tires finally found purchase, and Riley was thrown back against the passenger seat as the burly red minivan charged up the highway.

The bursts of gunfire died down in the distance as they crested a rise, Shepherd's men dropping out of sight as they awaited the inferno's embrace.

"How the fuck did we just pull that off!?" Sterling shouted, holstering his pistols as he craned his neck around to stare out through the shattered rear window.

"Pass the bottle," Hayden panted in exhilaration, grabbing the whiskey from Jesse. "I thought we were dead for sure."

"Power of positive thinking," Jesse tapped his temple – sage advice from a boozed-up bundle of sallow skin and bones.

"You've gotta teach me how to shoot like that some time," Riley gazed sidelong at Virge in breathless admiration.

"That lesson's gonna have to wait," he grinned triumphantly through his beard, one hand on the wheel, the other on the accelerator. "You owe me a couple new windows first."

"It was an ambush!" the walkie crackled with defeat in the center console, "Shooters in a red minivan heading east. They shot out our back tires. Request immediate assistance."

"Sorry, son," Shepherd's voice surfed over a wave of static. "We can't risk driving into another trap… You're gonna have to hoof it… All teams, and any survivors listening in – keep an eye out for raiders in a red minivan… Don't take any chances… Shoot on sight."

CHAPTER 21

"We need to ditch this car before we get spotted," Riley Armstrong sat up in the passenger seat, her eyes darting between the empty fields on either side of the highway.

They were clear of the forest now, but billowing black clouds of smoke blotted out the horizon as the bushfire blazed on behind them.

"Not a fucking chance," Virge Norton stared icily at the road ahead. "You think we're just gonna bump into another car like this on the road? I had to wait three months for this bitch to get built and shipped over from Michigan. And I doubt they're taking on any new orders these days."

Riley glanced over her shoulder for support, but Sterling was already snoring in the back, having hiked through the forest all night. Hayden and Jesse were both on the nod as well, the empty whiskey bottle rolling around between their feet.

"You heard Shepherd," she folded her arms. "Anybody who was listening to that broadcast is gonna be gunning for us now. We're as good as dead if we don't ditch it."

"And I'm as good as dead if we do," Virge clenched his jaw,

his knuckles turning white around the steering wheel. "No wheels, no home, no tomorrow. If we're forced to live off the land, I'll be the first to go, and you know it."

"That's not true," she furrowed her eyebrows at him. "You and Sterling are with us now, and we take care of our own. And if we're going up against Shepherd's people, we're gonna need each other."

"Yeah, my needs are bigger than yours though," he muttered as they drove across a long bridge.

Riley bit her bottom lip, unsure of what else she could say to sway him.

Peering at her side mirror, she could see that the bushfire was a safe distance behind them now. Or rather, it was far enough away to be considered less of an immediate danger than it was for them to stay on the highway in the red minivan.

"Okay, we won't ditch the car then," she finally relented, her shoulders dropping sympathetically as she looked back at Virge. "But we need to find a place to lay low for a while. We can't afford to be seen on the road."

"Way ahead of you," he squinted at a thicket of trees up ahead as he throttled back on the accelerator.

They turned down a long gravel road, the wall of trees on either side opening up to reveal a swaying sea of overgrown grass. A solitary homestead squatted at the end of the driveway, but Virge steered the minivan down a rutted trail instead, circling around the house towards a big metal hangar on the side of a small airstrip.

"How did you know about this place?" Riley asked as they pulled into a small concrete lot behind the hangar, parking beside a dusty silver sedan sitting in the shadow of a row of tilted solar panels.

"Local crop duster used to buy all his groceries at the truck stop," Virge replied, cracking open the driver's side door and unfolding his wheelchair. "He took me up a couple times just for the hell of it. Sold it all a while back though – moved down south to fly scenic tours along the coast."

"What about the new owners?" Riley climbed out of the minivan with almost as much trouble as Virge, pins and needles of pain shooting up her hands and thighs. She glanced over at the other three still asleep in the backseat before turning back to Virge, "Wouldn't they have seen us coming up the driveway?"

"Doubt it," he grunted as he reached across the driver's seat for his rifle and the walkie. "Some rich asshole was buying up all the land in the area before the world went to shit. He bought this place just to have somewhere to park his jet. If we don't see a plane in the hangar, it's safe to say it's just us out here."

They entered the gigantic metal shed through the back door, the cavernous garage echoing with Riley's footsteps.

Virge zoomed through the dimly lit gloom, fumbling with a shadowy switchboard in the corner.

Fluorescent lights flickered to life across the high ceiling, illuminating the big empty barn. Sliding bifold doors stood shut at the front of the hangar, with various workbenches and metal cupboards lining the walls. A half-finished wooden counter was gathering dust in the rear, alongside a stack of planks and cans of black paint.

"Just when I thought this place wouldn't have anything decent," Jesse Bowman croaked from the back door, his bloodshot eyes blearily focused on something behind the wooden counter. He staggered past paint brushes and boxes

122

of nails, nearly keeling over to snatch up an unopened bottle of cognac. Uncorking the brandy, he raised the bottle in a hollow toast, "Thank you, to whoever decided to build a bar in the back of a hangar."

"Are you serious, Jesse?" Riley frowned at him in disdain. "Was the whiskey not enough? Why are you so set on drinking yourself to death?"

"I don't know, *Riley*," he mocked her, taking a long pull before wiping his cracked lips with the back of his hand. "Have you ever had someone stab a needle full of meth into your arm? You don't think that fucks you up a little bit? Or how about driving halfway across the country just to find out that the people you've known for your entire life have just murdered both your parents?"

"Keith was your dad," she reminded him with ice in her voice.

"No, he lost that title," Jesse took an angry swig from the bottle, cognac spilling down his chin onto the rags of his soiled red shirt. "He should've lost it a long time ago. But when Susan stabbed my mom to death and he just shrugged it off – a fucking police officer shrugging off a murder – I knew how full of shit he was. He didn't give a flying fuck about me. None of you did. You all left me to bury her – by my fucking self!"

"You know why I wasn't gonna help you," Riley felt her blood boiling as she stared daggers at him, fury flowing down her forearm to form a fist, her bandaged fingers be damned. "Karen left with that son of a bitch Sinclair after he shot my dad, right in front of –"

"That was an accident," Jesse cut across her before taking another shaky pull from the bottle of brandy.

"They ran away!" Riley strode towards him, marching through the throb in her thighs. "Your mom watched Stuart shoot my dad and then they both left him to die. Accident or not, I sure wouldn't call them fucking innocent… But don't you *dare* try to tell me I didn't care about you. I set a place for you – right next to me – for every single meal at my grandma's house. Hayden and Greg tried to sit at the table with us a couple times, but Keith and I always said you might be coming. But you never even bothered to show up. *You're* the selfish prick who didn't give a shit about any of us!"

Jesse stared down at her trembling fist.

He didn't even move to defend himself.

He looked as though he was already broken.

Deep down, he probably would have welcomed the punch – just to feel something after having numbed himself to everything and everyone for so long.

Without a word, he turned away from her, trudging towards the back door, clutching his cognac like it was the only friend he had left in the world.

Watching him leave the hangar, Riley wondered whether she might have been too hard on him, but she shook herself out of it before the feeling could take hold.

With her father's death and her mother's kidnapping, both of her parents were gone as well, but at least she wasn't trying to use her troubles as an excuse to chase cheap thrills.

"Son of a bitch still owes me a bottle," Virge's voice echoed in the silence as he rolled from the far end of the big empty barn. He studied her face, his hard eyes softening. "Hey, you think the van's broken windows are gonna be an open invitation for any critters looking for somewhere to shit?"

"I don't know," Riley winced as her fist unfurled, her wounded fingers tender again as her angry adrenaline ebbed away.

"Everything okay in here?" Sterling appeared at the back door with Hayden in tow. "We heard yelling."

Both of them were weak with weariness, but while the dark circles underneath Sterling's eyes had stemmed from his all-night hike, Hayden was just hungover.

"Lover's spat," Virge remarked dryly with a sidelong smirk at Riley. At the sight of her death stare, he quickly added, "No, it was nothing. People get weird after a gunfight – as if these folks weren't weird enough."

"Where are we, Virge?" Sterling asked as he lumbered over to a nearby workbench, unfurling the map from the truck stop across the table.

"Just south of the river," the grizzled war veteran answered, joining him by the bench to trace his finger over to their new position. "Had to take the highway to get here, so we're still caught in between Lake Springworth and Long Plains – but that's exactly where we need to be, right?"

"Keep your enemies close," Riley agreed as she and Hayden gathered around the map. "So, what's our next move?"

"I don't think we should be attacking them again so soon," Hayden leaned one elbow on the workbench to hold his hungover head. "Shepherd's people are gonna be out in force now after that ambush. Besides, we don't have any water, we're down to chips and chocolate for food..." he paused for a moment, his eyes meeting Riley's, "And you need to take it easy, or you're just gonna wind up doing more damage to yourself."

"So, you wanna rest up for a while?" Sterling rubbed at his tired eyes with a yawn, almost as if he was talking to himself.

"My mom doesn't have *a while*," Riley reminded them all. She locked eyes with Hayden, "Neither do your friends." Then, turning to Sterling, she added, "And neither does your wife. Who knows what those men are doing to them right now, while we're just standing around here, bitching and moaning about what we don't have?"

Both Hayden and Sterling straightened up, galvanized by the wake-up call.

"Well, we don't have a plan either," Virge turned towards her, his eyebrows raised expectantly. He took the walkie from his lap and tossed it beside the map on the workbench. "We won't be able to lure them into another trap with the two-way either, so that's out."

"Why can't we just go in guns blazing?" she asked, staring down at the red circle around Lake Springworth. "We did just fine in our last two fire fights. There's no reason why we can't pull it off a third time. Hayden can drive while the three of us shoot."

"Here we go with this shit again," Virge grumbled to himself. He shot a scrutinizing squint at Sterling, "Granger, you wanna tell her why that's a bad idea?"

"We went over this back at the truck stop," Sterling pointed at the single road leading to the lake. "Their position's too strong. They've only got one access point to cover, and we don't know how many sentries they've got hidden in the forest."

"What about a hit-and-run then?" Riley furrowed her eyebrows as she studied the map. "We could cut through the trees on foot, take out a few of their guards overnight, and leave before they even find the bodies."

"Hit-and-run might work," Hayden supposed, before glancing pointedly at her legs, "But you can't run, remember?"

"Most forests don't have wheelchair ramps either," Virge grunted, brooding at chest-level height beside the bench.

"This isn't gonna work unless we're all mobile," Sterling affirmed, before tilting his head for a moment. He drew his finger northeast towards Burview, "But what if we took a back road to do a hit-and-run on the radio tower instead?"

"Just like we agreed on last time you brought this up," Virge crossed his arms and leaned back in his chair, "Shepherd's got that radio tower for his bait message locked up tight."

"But we've got a few more hands to help us now," Sterling replied, glancing at Riley and Hayden. "Besides, without the poultry farm's location, we don't really have much of a choice."

"Hold on a second," Riley's gaze slid south towards the red question mark on the map. "You don't know where the poultry farm is, but you know it's in Long Plains, right?"

"Somewhere around there, yeah," Virge answered as he leaned his elbows on the table, curious to hear what she was getting at.

"And there's only three highways heading south from the lake," she continued, pointing at the first roadway that ran alongside her grandmother's house. "This one's out for sure. And by the time that fire's done, the highway we're on now will be out as well," she traced one of her bandaged fingers towards the third road to the east. "So that just leaves this one. Even if the fire forces them to take the next nearest highway, they'll still have to circle back west to get to Long Plains."

"So we set up a trap along the road," Sterling concluded, tapping at the highway that ran east of Long Plains. He turned to Virge, "What do you think?"

"Cut their supply line," the old man nodded slowly, his eyebrows raised in subtle praise, "Guerrilla warfare, huh? Okay, depends on what kinda trap you're setting though."

"A barricade would be the easiest," Hayden chimed in, eager

to play a part in the plan. He made eye contact with Riley. "I've done this before. We set up a couple cars just over a hill, or around a bend, hit the windshield with some eggs," he paused, reconsidering the likelihood of finding eggs before glancing back at the half-finished bar counter, "Or a can of paint. Then we wait for them to crash into the barricade and let Virge pick off the survivors."

Riley flashed back to being dragged out of her family's red suburban on the freeway, lined up on her knees alongside her mother, Keith and Jesse.

The ambush had worked for Hayden and his friends back then.

But that was back when she had been stupid enough to fall for it.

"No," she said flatly, glancing at each of them in turn. "I don't wanna kill them. Not right away, at least. I wanna *distract* them. Let them call for help. And while Shepherd scrambles to send a second team to save their people on the highway," her gaze ran north along the map, "We'll be doing a hit-and-run in Burview."

"So we split up?" Sterling adjusted the hood of his green parka, his lips twisting, unconvinced. "Even if we can get that sedan outside to work, two of us are gonna need to take the van out on the road again. They'll spot us before we can even set the trap."

"Then we change the trap," Virge proposed, shifting in his seat, "Something they'll wreck their vehicle on, without us needing to be there to spring it. That way, we all stay together, and the van stays right here."

"We can't do the blockade then," Hayden folded his sinewy arms across his chest. "If we're not there to blind the windshield, we lose the shock factor, and they'll have too much time to react. As soon as they see the barricade, they'll slam the brakes."

"If we can find a tractor somewhere around here," Sterling ventured, peering at the map for likely tracts of farmland, "I could probably rig a plow and dig up a trench. Whoever's coming down that highway is gonna flip the fuck over."

"Fuck me, I thought we weren't trying to kill 'em," Virge grunted, sitting back in his chair again, his face shadowed with doubt. "Besides, you still need to find a tractor, find a plow, find some fuel, and put all the shit together. By the time you finally get that bitch down there, you're gonna miss their scheduled pick-up."

"What scheduled pick-up?" Riley furrowed her eyebrows at him.

"Once a week, they make a supply run down to Long Plains," he explained, nodding towards the walkie on the workbench as his source of information. "After tomorrow, you're looking at another week before they head down to the poultry farm again. And if they decide to clean up one of the highways that the bushfire knocked out in the meantime – well, we're shit outta luck."

Riley held his bleak gaze before turning her back on them all, taking a few faltering steps away from the table.

Another week for just a chance at hitting two birds with one stone, she contemplated, weighing up the consequences of each choice.

If they went with Hayden's blockade, they could take out at least two carloads of Shepherd's men. But then the rest of his people would be on high alert for any future attacks – and they'd be hard-pressed to find another opportunity for a stealth strike.

Sterling's trench, on the other hand, would give them enough time to prepare, scavenge some decent supplies and allow her to recover from her wounds. But at the same time, they'd be sentencing her mother and all of the other captive women to at least another week of brutality at the hands of Shepherd's men.

Staring around the hangar as if the right decision was written somewhere on the walls, her eyes fell to the unfinished bar.

Maybe Jesse had the right idea after all – catching a buzz was sure to take away some of her troubles, at least for a while.

"I've got an idea," she suddenly perked up, looking back over her shoulder at the other three. "We don't need a blockade or a trench. We can get this done tonight and be in Burview tomorrow. Hayden, go find Jesse."

CHAPTER 22

The *thock-thock-thock* of Hayden Marsh's hammering reverberated around the cavernous garage like gunfire.

Riley Armstrong was standing behind another workbench halfway across the hangar, although the metal walls made it sound as though he was banging nails right beside her.

Black paint sloshed over the table as she daubed her brush over a spiked plank of wood, coating it in obsidian.

Her bandaged fingers made clumsy work, but the job didn't have to be perfect.

By the time Shepherd's people would see the improvised spike strips, it would be too late.

She could picture it now – a group of errand boys driving along an unfamiliar route to Long Plains, grumbling about the extra travel time that the bushfire had tacked onto their weekly supply run, when their tires would explode underneath them, shredding on the camouflaged columns of nails, sparks flying from their screeching rims until they grated to a grinding halt.

"You feeling okay?" Hayden asked beside her as he slid a freshly spiked board onto her workbench.

"Huh?" Riley snapped out of her delightful daydream,

staring sidelong at him.

She had no idea how long he had been standing there.

Even now, she could still hear the echoes of his hammer halfway across the hangar, banging ghost nails into a plank of wood that apparently only existed in between her pounding eardrums.

And slowly but surely, as she held his gaze, she was becoming acutely aware of the broad smile that had been plastered plainly across her face.

"I think you need to take a break," Hayden decided quickly, grabbing the brush from her bandaged hand and plopping it back into the paint can. He took her gently by the arm and led her away from the workbench. "We probably should've found you a mask before we started. Those paint fumes can't have been good for you. Let's get you some fresh air."

"Paint fumes… good for… yeah, buddy," Riley slurred, her voice deep and unnatural in her own ears as Hayden hurried her towards the exit.

Her vision swam as they staggered over to the back door, the afternoon sun making the doorway shimmer in a bright rectangle that rotated from left to right and back again.

They stumbled outside, the first breath of fresh air sending Riley reeling to her hands and knees, dry heaving on the concrete as she battled waves of nausea.

Harsh white light blazed directly into her retinas from every angle, while vivid green blades of overgrown grass bent towards her, creeping ever closer every time she shut her eyes against the dazzling glare.

"Fuck, Virge!" Hayden yelled as his footfalls lumbered away.

Riley's skull rang with his panicked voice as she collapsed against the side of the hangar.

Fuck, Virge!

She cradled her throbbing head in her bandaged hands.

Fuck, Virge!

"… bring any fucking water," the old man muttered under his breath as he rolled to a stop beside her. He thrust a soda bottle in front of her face. "Here, drink this. Sip slow."

"Fuck, Virge!" Riley echoed before clumsily wrapping her hands around the bottle.

She spluttered on the first mouthful and spat out the second, taking a deep breath before swallowing the third.

Black splotches of paint on the back of her hands rose and fell as the harsh palette of her surroundings faded to a dull autumn day.

"Go check the house," Virge turned to Hayden. "I can't remember if there's a reservoir here but try the pipes anyway."

Feeling better with every breath, Riley set down the bottle, each puff of fresh air tasting as sweet as another sip of soda.

"What the hell just happened?" she panted, stealing a wary glance at the stalks of overgrown grass lining the concrete lot's edge.

"You gas chambered yourself," Virge replied, picking up the bottle of soda. "Come on. Get on your feet."

Riley struggled to plant one foot on the ground.

It felt as though her entire body was laden with lead.

"Fuck me," the old man grumbled, watching her with his scrutinizing squint. "Even I can stand up better than you."

She cocked her head at him, snorting at his half smile before thrusting her elbow into the wall, using it for leverage to bring her other foot underneath her.

"You look like a baby giraffe," he chuckled dryly. "Is this your first time?"

"Fuck you," she laughed with a pained grimace, doubling over at the waist with her bandaged hands on her knees, the ache of her strained groin coming back with a vengeance.

"That's good, hold that position," he took a swig from the soda bottle. "Get the air back into your lungs."

Riley's upper body heaved as she breathed deeply, coughing to expel the contaminants from her airways.

Only a short distance away, Sterling's snores from the backseat of the burly red minivan carried across the small concrete lot, the lone gunman garbed in green having slept through the entire ordeal.

Next to Virge's minivan, the hood of the dusty silver sedan was propped open, with Jesse's bottle of cognac lying beside the front tire.

"You should take it easy tonight," Virge decided as he screwed the bottle cap back on the soda. "I'll head down to Long Plains with Hayden. My chair can fit in the back of the sedan."

"No, I'm good," she insisted, despite wanting nothing more than to find a bed and curl up into a ball until morning. "I'll go."

"Your choice," he shrugged before studying her face for a moment. "You know something, you remind me of this one soldier I used to know. Real fuckhead. Stubborn as shit. Hated asking for help. Always pushed himself past his limits. Just an unstoppable force of pure fucking nature."

"What happened to him?" Riley asked, her breathing finally getting back under control.

"You're looking at him," the grizzled war veteran stared into her eyes, leaning forward in his wheelchair. "Listen, I know you wanna save your mom and the rest of your people. But you need to hear this – the human body can only bend so much until it breaks."

CHAPTER 23

"Virge!?" Hayden Marsh shouted as he sprinted around the corner with half a slab of bottled water cradled in his arm. "How is she?"

"She's fine," Riley straightened up, leaning back against the hangar's wall for support as he approached.

"Pipes don't work," Hayden reported as he fished a bottle from the plastic wrap and handed it to Riley, "But I found these in the garage."

"Good job, kid," Virge replied, waving off a bottle of water for himself. He eyed Riley for a moment longer before wheeling himself towards the hangar's back door, waiting for Hayden to follow. "Come on, show me what you've got left in there."

The two men disappeared inside as Riley lingered with her back against the wall, sipping slowly on the water, considering Virge's hard-learned advice.

She knew that she couldn't keep pushing herself like this forever.

Eventually, she would have to allow herself a chance to recover, or risk her body crashing at a time of its own choosing.

But she also knew that if the roles had been reversed, and she had been kidnapped while her mother had gotten away, Susan Armstrong would have stopped at nothing to rescue Riley from Shepherd's men.

There was no other choice – not if she ever wanted to look at her mother in the eye again.

She had to push through the pain for as long as it took.

A slam from the dusty silver sedan jerked Riley back to her senses.

"Where's Virge?" Jesse looked up from the hood of the car.

"Inside," she answered stiffly, finding herself wishing that she had followed the other two back into the hangar.

Despite having asked Jesse to get the sedan working again, she couldn't stand the sight of the scrawny alcoholic wretch.

"Well, I hooked up the battery from the van," he nodded at the discarded dead battery on the ground, before ambling around the side of the dusty silver sedan. Snatching up his bottle of cognac from beside the front tire, he added, "You should be good to go."

"Are you sure you're even sober enough to put the cables on the right way?" she narrowed her eyes at him as he took a pull from the bottle.

"You can check for yourself," Jesse shrugged, wiping his cracked lips with the back of his hand. "Keys are in the visor."

She begrudgingly faltered forward towards the car, when the *thock-thock-thock* of Hayden's hammering resumed, reverberating around the walls of the hangar.

"Riley," Virge appeared in the doorway beside her, shooting Jesse a scrutinizing squint. "Come with me for a minute. Need you to do something for me before I can let you and Hayden go tonight."

"Let us go?" she echoed in confusion, following him around the side of the hangar. "You said it was *my choice* whether I wanna go or not."

"It still is – I'm not gonna get in your way," he grunted over his shoulder as he trundled through the overgrown grass. "Your hands are fucked. Your legs are fucked. Your head's probably fucked as well – especially after breathing in all those fumes. But it's your life, your decision. What I won't do though, is let you put Hayden's life on the line if you're not in a position to protect him."

"What do you mean?" Riley asked as they stopped short of the small airstrip.

"Here," Virge handed her a pistol, "One of Granger's. He's out like a light. He won't even know it's gone until you're back." The grizzled war veteran pointed out the empty whiskey bottle that he had placed on the other side of the runway. "If you can hit that bottle from here, I'll let Hayden go with you tonight. If not – stiff shit – you can set up the trap by yourself. Or you can stay here and I'll go with Hayden instead."

Riley stared down at the gun in her hands.

She had held her father's pistol a hundred times, but Sterling's felt heavier.

The weight was similar enough, but the consequence of missing the target was an unnecessary burden on her shoulders.

She flipped the safety lever off, supposing that the consequences would be much worse if she missed her shot against a real threat.

Like that fat sack of shit that killed Keith, she remembered ruefully, the weight of the weapon disappearing.

Drawing herself into a fighter's stance, turning at the waist with her left foot forward and right foot back, Riley gritted her teeth as she awkwardly curled her bandaged fingers around the pistol's hilt.

She lined up her sights on the bottle, both hands shaking slightly as she applied small increments of pressure on the trigger.

CRACK!

The bullet ricocheted off the runway, ripping a gash through the concrete as it bounced up into the tall grass on the other side, leaving the whiskey bottle wobbling in its wake, but still unbroken.

"Stiff shit, I guess," Virge supposed, spinning his chair towards her. "Want some advice?"

"Sure, why not," Riley replied with her shoulders slumped.

"If you crouch, you won't shake as much," he nodded at her bandaged hands knowingly, "Makes you a smaller target too. And don't tilt your head down. Bring the sights up to your eye level."

She held his gaze for a moment before refocusing on the bottle.

Gasping in pain from her strained groin as she sank down on one knee, she rested her left elbow on top of her thigh, pulling the pistol up until she was staring along the top of the barrel.

"Keep your gun on the target after you take the shot," Virge continued as he turned his attention back towards the bottle again. "You wouldn't drop your weapon if you missed your mark in a fire fight, would you?"

Riley lined up her sights again, her hands stiff but steady.

CRACK!

The whiskey bottle's neck exploded, the rim snapping off as shards of glass showered the other side of the runway.

"Thanks," she breathed, keeping her aim on the bottle for a few more seconds before flipping the safety lever back on. "And here I was thinking you weren't gonna teach me how to shoot until we found a way to fix up your broken windows."

"Don't remind me," he grumbled as he watched her struggle to her feet again. "I just figured, if you can't kill someone from a distance, you're probably gonna get one of us killed when we hit Burview tomorrow. Good luck out there tonight."

CHAPTER 24

"I gotta say," Riley Armstrong sat in the front passenger seat of the dusty silver sedan, "You made it sound like a bad thing when you said we're down to chips and chocolate for food."

She popped another potato chip into her mouth, savoring the taste of salt and vinegar before crunching the crispy crinkle-cut slice. She knew that the junk food was just empty calories with next to no nutritional content, but after months of living off pine nuts, game meat, and Grandma Eleanor's vegetable garden, she certainly wasn't complaining.

"You're unbelievable," Hayden grinned behind the steering wheel. "You know there was some canned food back in that house too, right?"

"And I'll eat that as well," she assured him around her mouthful, "I just don't see any point in letting these go to waste."

He chuckled to himself as they hurtled towards the twilit horizon on the highway, searching for a suitable location for setting up the spike trap.

They had already turned east from the rural blink-and-you'd-miss-it town of Long Plains.

Black smoke rose high over the vast empty prairies away on their left, Grandma Eleanor's final spark of life still raging on across the Nebraskan countryside, burning in an orange glow of defiance against the approaching night sky.

"Not looking too good so far," Hayden remarked as they passed by a derelict cluster of farm silos and warehouses.

He was right.

The highway was too perfect to lay a trap.

The road was too flat for them to plant the spiked boards behind a rise, and the few curves that they had come across were too wide to surprise any approaching vehicles that might come speeding around a corner.

There was only one thing that could work in their favor – Shepherd's men would most likely be thundering down the highway, since there was literally nothing else on the road that they would need to slow down for.

"Look at it this way," Riley tried to remain optimistic, "We're more likely to be successful the farther east we go. Who knows how far away this poultry farm is from Long Plains?"

"Yeah, I guess," he replied, unconvinced as he stared at the empty stretch of road ahead. "As long as we don't go so far east that we pass the highway they'll be coming down."

"Well, at least it's not a blockade," Riley smirked at him as she tied off the packet of chips and stowed it into the glove box for later. "They would've seen that coming from a couple miles away."

They drove in silence for a while, dusk settling in over the wide open plains.

Hayden flicked on the headlights, still scanning for a likely location where their row of spike strips wouldn't be spotted so easily.

Dull gleams of weathered paint glinted softly in the darkness on one side of the highway, with hulking farm machinery and forgotten bales of hay sprawled out across a field.

With the rows of tractors for sale lining the road, Riley found herself thinking that Sterling's trench might not have been such a bad idea after all, although they still would have been hard-pressed to figure out a way to disguise a giant hole in the highway.

Faint patches of stars struggled to shine in the evening sky, with haze from the wildfire blending into the long clouds reaching across the deep violet canvas.

"We're running outta road here, Riley," Hayden finally broke the silence, putting their dreaded thoughts into words. "What if we don't find somewhere to set up the trap?"

"Then we drop some spike strips anyway," she gazed out into the night, not wanting to miss a thing while he had his crisis of confidence. "Maybe they'll think there's a couple snakes on the highway. Besides, what else are we gonna do with all these boards in the back?"

"Do you really think this plan's gonna work though?" he began to voice his doubts. "I mean, even if they do run over the spike strips and radio back to base for help. What if Shepherd just tells them he's not gonna risk letting anyone else drive into an ambush, just like he did with those guys back at the truck stop?"

"It doesn't make a fucking difference," Riley bristled in her seat. It was as if he had already accepted defeat. "Whether Shepherd sends all of his men to find out who's been fucking with them, or the people doing the supply run just take a back road to Long Plains and we end up doing all this shit for nothing – regardless of what happens, we'll be in Burview tomorrow, doing a hit-and-run on that radio tower."

"If you say so," Hayden exhaled in resignation, slowing down as they passed a wildlife crossing sign.

They followed a slight bend around another infuriatingly wide corner, a thicket of trees soon looming out of the darkness on either side of the highway.

"Stop the car," Riley sat up as the road straightened out again.

"I'm sorry, you're right, I shouldn't have –"

"Forget it," she cut across his attempt to apologize, looking back over her shoulder. "You just – shut up. Turn around. We're here."

"This isn't a good spot though," he replied, pumping the brakes all the same. He spun the steering wheel over to the other side of the highway to turn the car around. "The curve's too wide. They'll see it straight away."

"They're gonna see the trap wherever we put it," Riley reminded him as they reversed out of the gravel shoulder. "At least here, we've got a chance of them ignoring it."

"Ignoring it?" Hayden echoed in confusion, shifting the gearstick back into drive.

"Right here," she leaned forward with her elbows on the dashboard, studying the stretch of road in front of them, "Stop, stop, stop."

"You want it *here?*" he asked incredulously, glancing up at the rearview mirror as he pulled up the handbrake. "Riley, we're on the wrong side of the corner. They'll be coming from this side, remember? We need to follow the bend, at least for a little while longer."

"Trust me, this is the spot," she cracked open the passenger door, gritting her teeth through the pain in her strained groin as she climbed out onto the road. "Let's go. Bring one of the boards."

Hayden followed her uncertainly as she walked in between the headlights' beams, inspecting a twin set of skids along the asphalt, the streaks of burnt rubber twisting like a pair of black scars across the highway.

"Looks like somebody ignored the wildlife crossing sign," Riley supposed, standing to one side to let the idling car's headlamps light up the road. She looked over at the painted plank of nailed wood in Hayden's hand, "See if you can line it up along the tracks."

He laid the spiked board along the nearest tire mark as best as he could, both ends sticking out from the curve of the skid like a pair of sore thumbs.

But it didn't have to look perfect – at least not from this distance.

"Not bad," Hayden admitted, stepping back to see how well the painted spike strip blended in with the black streak of burnt rubber. "It's a lot better than hoping they'll think there's a couple snakes on the highway."

Working under the misty light of the moon and the head-lamps' beams, they laid their trap across the road, with Hayden carrying the planks of wood from the backseat of the dusty silver sedan, while Riley gently kicked and nudged them all into position.

"Do you think they're okay?" Hayden asked as he dropped another plank at her feet. "I mean your mom, Chelsea, Katanya… Lorraine."

"They fucking better be," Riley clenched her jaw as she toed the nailed board into place, "I don't wanna think about what I'm gonna do to Shepherd if they're not."

"Same here," he agreed, looking up at the faint orange

glow rising over the treetops, the wildfire still burning in the distance. "I just wanna make it up to them, you know? For not being there this morning. Maybe you were right – maybe I could've made a difference if I was out there, instead of hiding down in the wine cellar."

"Or maybe you could've gotten yourself killed," she sighed, finally allowing herself to see the sense in him staying out of sight. "Just like my grandma, Keith and Greg."

"I really hope this plan works," Hayden locked eyes with her. He dusted his hands before turning back towards the sedan. "I can't wait to catch those fuckers off guard tomorrow."

"It's gonna work," Riley affirmed as she took a moment to admire the array of spike strips. Then, in a smaller voice, she added, "It has to work."

Just as she finished her sentence, a twig snapped in the thicket of trees on the north side of the highway.

Riley's pupils dilated at the noise, grappling with the unsettling feeling that they were being watched.

CHAPTER 25

Riley Armstrong instinctively drew Sterling's pistol from the waistband of her jeans at the small of her back.

Flipping off the safety lever and cradling the gun in her bandaged hands, she scanned the thicket of trees for signs of movement.

Halfway back towards the dusty silver sedan, Hayden Marsh stopped in his tracks, listening for any other sounds.

The idling car's headlights stopped at the gravel shoulder, forcing them to rely on the moonlight to peer into the darkness.

Autumn leaves rustled in the wind as Riley backed away from the spike trap.

"Probably a deer," Hayden shrugged after a while. "It's a wildlife crossing, remember?"

"Shut up," she shushed him, still scanning the trees.

That's when she saw it.

A big pair of yellow eyes stalking them from the shadows, reflecting the moonlight, but only for a moment as a cloud floated across the sky, wreathing them in darkness.

"Get back to the car," she urged, pointing her pistol at the forest. "Don't run."

"What is it?" he whispered back, slowly sidestepping towards the sedan. "Did you see something?"

CRACK!

She fired a warning shot into the trees.

Something snarled menacingly in response.

Something big.

The cloud cleared the moon, and the pair of yellow eyes shone again.

An icy bolt of adrenaline surged through Riley's veins as she watched a muscular mountain lion emerge from the thicket.

"Fucking hell," Hayden froze, staring in horror at the stealthily advancing cougar.

The big cat continued its slow silent gait towards the highway, softly pawing over the gravel shoulder as its keen eyes flicked back and forth between them.

"Hayden, get back to the car," Riley repeated, the pistol shaking in her hands as she lined up her sights on the stalking mountain lion.

Virge's advice to steady her aim by crouching was useless when faced with a cougar.

Contrary to an enemy holding a gun, Riley knew that if she made herself smaller, to a mountain lion, she would only become a bigger target.

"What about you?" Hayden swallowed nervously, staring back at the big cat.

The mountain lion lowered itself to the asphalt, all four of its muscular legs coiled into powerful springs, its long tail twitching from side to side.

"I'll be fine," Riley breathed, bringing the gun up to eye level and taking aim at the predator's skull.

CRACK!

The bullet ripped through the night air, only to graze the animal's cheek as the cougar snapped its head towards the sound.

Enraged, the mountain lion hissed against the pain, baring its fangs at Riley as it shifted its ferocious feline body towards her, preparing to pounce.

Her heart racing a mile a minute, Riley kept her gun trained on the target, fear forcing her to overcome her shaky hands as she slowly squeezed the trigger again.

"Over here, you big fucking pussy!" Hayden yelled, stooping to snatch up one of the spiked planks on the road.

"HAYDEN, NO!!" Riley shouted as the cougar jerked its gaze towards him, her next shot punching into the animal's big dense shoulder with dismal effect.

Before Hayden could stand upright, the savage predator seized the opportunity to attack, launching itself towards him, closing half the distance in a single leap.

In the blink of an eye, its forelegs were already off the asphalt again as the mountain lion lunged for Hayden's throat, claws drawn and jaws gaping wide.

Another cold spike of adrenaline pumped through Riley's bloodstream, slowing time down to a standstill.

The ferocious cougar was frozen in the air between them, reaching for Hayden with its monstrous paws, a natural-born killer surging towards its next meal.

Hayden didn't stand a chance holding the spiked board.

He was about to touch the reaper, winding up for a baseball swing that would never connect in time.

Riley's sights were wobbling as she traced the beast's trajectory with the gun barrel, the slightest lapse in her aim meaning the difference between bringing down the animal or shooting Hayden square in the chest.

Faced with the split second decision, she knew that she couldn't risk taking the shot.

She couldn't risk killing him.

But she didn't have a choice.

He was dead if she didn't pull the trigger.

The pistol barked in her hands, sending a hot slug rippling through the air, rocketing towards the leaping mountain lion and burrowing into the back of its neck.

Despite the well-placed shot, the cougar was still on course for Hayden's throat, its razor-sharp claws mere inches from tearing into the side of his neck.

Her bandaged hands jolting from the recoil, Riley refocused her aim, leveling the gun's barrel again before the empty shell casing could even hit the ground.

Another bullet took flight, hurtling towards its target.

Hayden's eyes were wide with terror, staring into the beast's maw.

The mountain lion's head snapped backwards, its entire ferocious feline body turning stiff in mid-air as the lead round bored a hole through the base of its skull.

Time sped up again as the felled beast came down on top of Hayden, the cougar's dead weight knocking him to the ground.

Riley kept her gun trained on the animal, venturing closer to confirm the kill.

Draped across Hayden, with its glassy yellow eyes staring lifelessly into the headlights of the idling dusty silver sedan, the dead mountain lion looked as peaceful as an overgrown house cat lazing in the sun.

"Hey, you okay?" she asked, flipping the pistol's safety lever on before sliding it into the waistband of her jeans at the small of her back.

Groaning in a haze of shock and relief, Hayden struggled out from underneath the cougar's carcass, yowling in agony every time he shoved at the animal's bloodstained fur.

"I think I broke a rib," he wheezed, kicking himself out from underneath the beast's body. He winced as he stretched one arm towards Riley, "Help me up?"

She stared down at him, unable to move.

"Oh, that's right, your hands," Hayden rolled over onto his knees before lumbering to his feet, blood dripping from his woolen jumper onto the asphalt. He glanced up at Riley again, "What's wrong?"

"Your…" she could barely form the words, her voice stuck in her throat.

In its final moments, the savage cougar had raked its razor-sharp claws across Hayden's chest, with four diagonal gashes running from his shoulder down to his hip.

CHAPTER 26

"We need to get this thing off the road," Hayden Marsh stared down at the mountain lion lying dead in the middle of the highway, completely oblivious to the four bloody slashes across his torso. "If Shepherd's people see it, they'll slow down for sure."

"No, we need to get back to the hangar," Riley Armstrong started towards the idling dusty silver sedan, "Right now."

"Relax, it'll only take a minute," Hayden hunched over the cougar's carcass, seizing it by the tail and dragging it away with a pained grimace. "Otherwise we've done all this for nothing. Could you fix up that board?"

He was right and wrong at the same time.

If they didn't stop to clean up the highway now, Shepherd's men would steer clear of the trap tomorrow, hindering all of their efforts to sabotage the raiders' operations and distract them before the hit-and-run on Burview.

On the other hand, every second that passed by brought Hayden an inch closer to death.

Riley's father had died due to blood loss three months ago now, and she couldn't stand the thought of watching somebody else she cared about crawling to an early grave – not if she could prevent it.

But Hayden was already at the gravel shoulder, and besides, completing the mission meant that they had a greater chance of rescuing her mother.

Resolved to finish what they had started, Riley stooped to fix up the spike strip, the pain of her strained groin reigniting as if to admonish her for casting her morals aside – however fleetingly short.

"Oh, fuck me," Hayden's inevitable cry of alarm came from the side of the road. "Riley, I think this is my blood. I think I'm fucking bleeding."

"Shit, we need to go," she lurched to her feet, feigning her shock as he staggered back towards the car. "Get in the passenger seat, I'll drive."

"Fuck, this is bad," he stared down at the red rags of his woolen jumper, his pupils dilating at the extent of his injuries. "This is really fucking bad."

"Just get in the fucking car, Hayden!" she shouted, throwing the passenger side door open and shoving him inside.

Riley limped around to the other side of the sedan, jumping in behind the steering wheel and punching the gearstick into drive before gunning the engine, narrowly avoiding the snaking strings of spike strips on the road.

"I'm – I'm losing too much blood," Hayden sputtered, his eyes widening in horror as he gaped at his hands covered in crimson. "We're not gonna make it back in time... I'm not gonna make it."

"Don't you fucking come at me with your negative bullshit right now!" Riley yelled as she floored the pedal down the highway. "You just hauled a grown-ass cougar off the road less than a minute ago. You're fine! You're gonna be fine!!"

"I dunno, Riley, I don't –"

"Stop, just stop," she cut across his uncertainty as they thundered through the night. Breathing out her anxiety, she took on a tender tone, trying to soothe his nerves, "Just, please – put your seat back, relax, and stop talking. Try to put some pressure on it. I'm gonna get you back to the hangar and we'll get you fixed up, okay?"

Hayden glanced sidelong at her before sinking back in the passenger seat.

He gingerly patted his hands along the length of his wound for a moment, before reaching into the backseat for one of the nailed boards instead, hugging the smooth side of the plank against his torso with a grunt of pain.

Riley kept her eyes fixated on the highway as she listened to his groans.

She knew that making him believe that he was going to survive the cougar's claws was half the battle, giving him enough hope to hang onto while she fought the other half – getting him back in time to treat his wound.

Riley had no idea whether Virge, Sterling and Jesse were even capable of helping Hayden, but she had to try.

She had to put her faith into the thought that they could patch him up and bring him back to health – just as much as Hayden had to believe it.

They didn't have any other choice with his life hanging in the balance.

CHAPTER 27

Riley Armstrong blared the dusty silver sedan's horn as they rumbled down the rutted trail in between the swaying seas of overgrown grass.

The hulking metal hangar was swathed in darkness, the light of the moon hidden behind a veil of smoky haze.

Mounting the small concrete lot behind the somber plane shed, their tires screeched to a stop beside Virge's burly red minivan.

The hangar's back door opened a crack, with dim flickering light spilling forth from inside, followed by the barrel of a hunting rifle.

"Virge!" Riley shouted as she set foot on the concrete, glancing sidelong at Hayden's ashen face in the front passenger seat. "Come quick, we need help!"

The back door swung wide, and Virge emerged with his rifle lying across his lap.

"Took your time out there!" he yelled, wheeling himself towards the car. "We thought you'd been captured. What the hell happened?"

The grizzled war veteran got his answer the moment he

drew up alongside the sedan, staring through the glass at Hayden slumped in the passenger seat.

"Granger!" he roared over his shoulder as he yanked open the car door, "Get your ass out here, double-time!!"

"We got attacked by a mountain lion," Riley explained as she limped around the side of the sedan, with a frustrated feeling that she was merely stating the obvious. "He's lost a lot of blood."

"Hey, what's going –" Sterling stopped mid-sentence in the plane shed's doorway, holstering his pistol as he rushed over to help.

Hayden's chin lolled onto his chest as Sterling slid an arm underneath him, scooping the former college footballer up out of the passenger seat.

Draping Hayden's sinewy arm over his shoulders, Sterling lugged him back towards the hangar, staggering underneath his weight, with both Riley and Virge unable to do anything other than follow them inside.

Jesse was swaddled in a blanket in the center of the giant shed, dozing beside a wheelbarrow bonfire, surrounded by dining chairs and mattresses scavenged from the property's solitary homestead.

"Get him on the workbench!" Virge barked as he zoomed past Sterling, sweeping his arm across the table and sending their supplies crashing to the floor, "Riley, first aid kit!"

"Is he gonna be okay?" she asked in a small voice, staring down at Hayden's blue lips as he gazed up at the ceiling in a silent trance.

"That depends on whether you can get me the fucking first aid kit!" Virge's voice echoed in the cavernous garage as he wheeled his legs underneath the bench. He held the back of his hand over Hayden's mouth, feeling his shallow breaths. "We don't have much time."

"Let's get this off him," Sterling leaned over the table to grab hold of Hayden's collar, preparing to rip the red rags of his tattered woolen jumper straight down the middle.

"No, you idiot!" Virge knocked his arms away with a swift backhand, "You'll peel the fucking scab off and he'll start bleeding out again. Get me some water!"

Sterling fell to the floor beside Riley, almost bashing their heads against each other in their haste as they searched through their scattered supplies.

Scavenged canned food rolled in every direction as they tossed aside packets of chips and chocolate.

"About damn time," Virge grumbled as Riley handed him the first aid kit.

Seizing a pair of scissors out of the box, the old war veteran began cutting away Hayden's jumper and shirt, taking care to avoid the patches of dried blood in the dim light from the bonfire. He had to make two separate cuts, one on either side of the four diagonal slashes running from Hayden's shoulder down to his hip.

"Alright, let's get that water now," Virge gestured for Sterling to come forward with what remained of the plastic bottles, "*Slowly*."

Together, they peeled strips of wet fabric from the caked crimson across Hayden's chest, careful to keep his fresh scab intact.

The former college footballer barely made a noise, although he had been unresponsive ever since Riley had peeled around the highway's intersection to speed north from Long Plains.

She turned away from the grisly scene on the table to see

Jesse tottering up from behind, carrying a blazing firebrand in one hand and yet another bottle of cognac in the other.

"That's good, hold that light," Virge muttered over his shoulder as they worked.

"Should I pour some of this on him?" Jesse asked, offering them the brandy.

"Water's better," Sterling answered stiffly, tossing a bloody ribbon of fabric onto the floor.

"No point in wasting a good drink," Virge grunted in agreement, turning around to grab the bottle and taking a big swig. He pushed himself away from the table, shaking his head at Hayden's glassy eyes, "He's fucked."

"You can't just give up on him," Riley glared at Virge before snatching the cognac out of his grasp.

"Come on, he's just a kid," Sterling took her side, tilting his head as he studied the contents of the first aid kit. "There's gotta be something we can do for him."

"Yeah, we could end his suffering," Virge scowled at the bottle of brandy in Riley's hand.

"That's not happening," she cocked her head at the old man. "What else can we do?"

"Okay, I'll tell you what he needs," he grumbled, eyeing the three of them in turn. "He's gonna need a blood transfusion to stop his organs from shutting down – that's if they haven't already started going. Anyone here know their blood type?"

They glanced at each other before shaking their heads.

"Doesn't matter, because we don't have the fucking equipment anyway," he continued, brooding in his chair. "Next problem – we need to close the wound. If it was just one scratch, I'd try sewing him up and call it a day. Two, sure, but the stitches would be tighter than a virgin's ass. Four though? Fuck yourself, no chance. They'd rip open every time he moved... And on top of all that, I'd probably fuck it up anyway. I'm not a damn doctor."

An unbidden image of Doctor Stuart Sinclair flew into Riley's mind – begging for his life on his knees, claiming that the whole world was about to change, and that they were going to need his help.

As much as she didn't want to accept the hard truth of Sinclair's final words, she couldn't deny that having a doctor around would have helped immensely right now – even if he was just a plastic surgeon.

"What if we cook the wound shut?" Jesse suggested, holding his firebrand aloft.

"Better than stitches," Virge shrugged, although there was no change in his bleak tune, having already considered cauterization, "But if there's any infection in there, we'd be sealing it in. We burn his wound shut now, and in a couple days, he'll burn up from the inside out."

"Then we fucking duct tape him back together," Riley snapped, pushing past Sterling to dig through the first aid kit, holding up a coil of surgical tape.

"Knock yourselves out," Virge replied, reaching forward to take the bottle of cognac off her hands. "But without that blood transfusion, you're just wasting your time."

"We'll fucking see, won't we?" she gave him a death stare before struggling to find the end of the tape with her clumsy fingers, holding it closer to the light of Jesse's firebrand.

"Here," Sterling plucked the tape from her bandaged hands, nodding towards Hayden. "Push his skin together."

Riley swallowed her wave of nausea as the weight of his instruction hung in the air.

159

Planting her palms on Hayden's shoulder, she gently pressed his flesh in from either side of the four claw marks.

"Hang in there, Hayden," she breathed, determined to keep him alive, even as he stared senselessly up at the ceiling.

CHAPTER 28

Riley Armstrong jerked awake at the drumming sound of wood on metal.

She attempted to stretch from her sleep, but the pain of her strained groin was somehow even worse than it had been yesterday. Their frantic escape from the bushfire hadn't helped either, her whole body aching after pinballing down the mountainside.

Blinking hard, she wiped her eyes with her bandaged fingers, finding herself curled up on a mattress beside the remains of last night's bonfire.

Sterling Granger stood over the wheelbarrow, stoking the embers as he added another scrap of wood to the rust-covered bucket.

"Back to life, huh?" he offered her a thin smile as a puff of smoke blew towards him.

"Feels more like death," she groaned, struggling upright to warm her hands by the fledgling flames. Her weary eyes lit up suddenly, "Where's Hayden? How is he?"

"Doing better than last night," Sterling replied, nodding towards another mattress on the other side of the wheelbarrow.

161

Gritting her teeth against the grating pain, Riley clambered to her feet to see Hayden sleeping on his back, wrapped up in a puffy black jacket.

Jesse was kneeling by his side, trickling the dregs of a plastic water bottle into his mouth.

"Are we sure that's water?" she asked suspiciously, narrowing her eyes at Jesse, despite the healthy shade of color that had returned to Hayden's face overnight.

"Good one," Jesse croaked, staring back at her with his red-rimmed eyes, still holding the bottle over Hayden's lips. "I'd laugh, but I'm too busy making sure he gets what's left of my share of the water."

"You're... being helpful?" Riley furrowed her eyebrows at him in disbelief.

"It's the least I can do," he shrugged, tossing the empty bottle aside. "He was the one who helped me up the mountain behind your grandma's house. I probably wouldn't have made it over the ridge otherwise... Besides, water's not really my thing nowadays."

The hangar's back door slammed shut as Virge rolled in, a flurry of ash swirling around his chair and settling on his shoulders.

"Bushfire's run its course," he reported, scratching his beard. He looked over at Hayden lying down on the mattress beside the wheelbarrow. "Is he gonna be ready to move?"

"He's stable, but..." Sterling faltered, stepping away from the smoke of the crackling bonfire, "I don't think he's in any condition to come with us to Burview."

"Well then, someone's gonna have to stay behind to watch him," Virge grumbled, moving towards the map draped over the unfinished bar counter.

"Is that you volunteering?" Riley asked, sharing an uncertain glance with the other two.

"Did it sound like I was volunteering?" his baritone voice dripped with disdain. He looked back over his shoulder as he reached the counter, "In case you've forgotten, my van's battery is in the sedan now – and after what happened to you two last night, I've decided I'm not going anywhere without it from now on."

"What happened last night was an accident," Riley replied, her shoulders squaring up. She had been expecting this argument with him from the moment that the mountain lion's attack was over. She had no doubt that Virge held her directly responsible for not being able to protect Hayden. She jerked her head over towards the bloodstained workbench, "But you wanted to let Hayden die on that table. That wasn't an accident. That was intentional."

"I'm not talking about what happened to Hayden!" his booming voice reverberated around the cavernous garage. He took a measured breath, turning his chair around to face her. "You made the right call, patching him up. Good for you. But if you hadn't survived that cougar attack – if the two of you went down on that highway last night, both of you would be dead right now. And then what would've happened to the rest of us?"

He glanced pointedly at Sterling and Jesse.

"We would've been fine," Sterling answered on Riley's behalf, not quite understanding what Virge was getting at. "I mean, we're no worse off here than where we were back at the truck stop, but we'd get by."

"That's right, *we* would've been fine," Virge echoed, locking eyes with Sterling, "Because I would've sent you to go fetch another car battery to get us on the road again." He turned back to Riley, "But if I have to stay behind today, and the three of you don't come back from Burview, who the fuck am I gonna send out for supplies? Hayden?"

"We're coming back," Riley replied, as if saying it out loud would ensure their success. "It's a hit-and-run. By the time they realize they're under attack, we'll be long gone."

"You guys go," Jesse's hoarse voice piped up, still kneeling beside Hayden. "I'll stay with him. I'd probably just get in the way out there anyway."

"No, I need you with us," Riley said firmly. The words sounded strange in her own ears, especially when referring to Jesse, but he had surprisingly begun to make himself useful for a change. She glanced at the other two in turn, "If we're planning on doing some real damage in Burview, Jesse has to be there."

He looked up at her with a mixture of gratitude and redemption in his red-rimmed eyes, along with an uncertainty of whether he had heard her correctly.

"Well, don't look at me," Sterling frowned back at the three of them. "I'm the only one here who can still run and gun. That's if you don't want them hearing us pulling up in the car. And besides, you're gonna need a local behind the wheel if you're planning on taking the back roads." He jerked his thumb over at Virge, "Him giving you directions from the passenger seat isn't gonna cut it. If you hit the wrong ditch – and there's plenty wrong around here – congratulations, you're walking home."

"I think it's pretty clear who needs to stay behind," Virge raised his eyebrows at Riley. "Your injuries are almost as bad as Hayden's. Both of you should stay here to recover while we handle the radio tower. You're just gonna slow us down otherwise."

"Rest today, fight tomorrow," Sterling agreed, offering a sympathetic nod in her direction.

"*Me!?*" she asked incredulously, shifting her weight to glance sidelong at the other two.

As if in response to her question, a sharp twinge of pain pulled at her strained groin.

"I know from experience, that's the last thing you wanna hear," Sterling rubbed at the dark circles underneath his eyes. "It's not easy. They killed my brother and took my Abbie. Every day that's gone by without a fight has been fucking torture. But Virge convinced me to hold off. Wait until we're ready, and then hit them with everything we've got."

"You wanna hit them with everything?" Riley cocked her head to the side, "What do you think I'm gonna do when we get there, lie down and surrender? I'll kill them all with my bandaged fucking hands if I have to!"

"I have no doubt that you would," Sterling picked his next words carefully. "But you don't wanna make this your last fight. We've still got a long ways to go. All we're saying is, hang back on this one, you'll get your day soon... Besides, you saw me in Clementine – I've got enough fury in me to fucking bury Burview just on my own."

"So we're leaving the wounded to take care of the wounded," Jesse croaked beside Hayden. "Are we sure that's a good idea?"

"Don't have any other choice," Virge grumbled as he continued to stare at Riley, waiting for her to accept the truth.

The human body can only bend so much until it breaks, she swallowed as the grizzled war veteran's hard-earned lesson echoed in her ears.

They were right.

She had been pushing herself too far for too long.

Even now, merely standing on her feet after a long night's rest was beginning to take its toll, the tight tendons in her thighs and hips filing away at her pelvis.

Reluctantly accepting her weakness, she was about to sink back down onto her mattress again when Hayden stirred awake.

"Nobody's bothered to ask me yet," he murmured from the other side of the wheelbarrow bonfire.

"Hey, take it easy," Jesse tried to hold him down, but the former college footballer brushed his hand aside.

"I'm coming with you," Hayden propped himself up on one elbow with a pained grimace. "I wanna watch Shepherd's people pay for what they did to our friends. I wanna hear them scream, I wanna see them run, and I wanna smell their blood in the streets when we gun them all down." He locked eyes with Riley, "And Miss Cougar Killer needs to be there too… because from what I saw in Clementine, Sterling can't aim for shit."

He collapsed back onto his mattress with a dry chuckle that soon turned into a groan of agony.

"Fucking ass-monkey," Virge wheeled himself over to the bonfire, studying Hayden with a scrutinizing squint. "You're gonna reopen your fucking wound out there."

"Yeah, but it's his choice," Jesse shrugged, staggering to his feet.

"And mine," Riley steeled herself, drawing strength from the mauled man's resolve.

"Well, we can't delay the attack," Sterling reminded them all. "Shepherd's men are gonna hit that spike trap today, and I'm not waiting another week for their next supply run. My Abbie doesn't have that long. If she doesn't get her meds soon…"

"For fuck's sake," Virge muttered under his breath, "Am I the only one around here –"

A wave of static from the black walkie beside the map on the bar counter cut him off.

"Base, come in!" a panicked voice yelled over the radio, "Our truck just rolled over on the new route to the chicken coop. Oh fuck, there's blood everywhere. Send help!!"

The static died down again as Riley, Virge, Sterling and Jesse stared around at each other before looking down at Hayden.

"We're on," Riley declared, flexing her bandaged fingers as she headed towards the door.

CHAPTER 29

Nebraska's back roads were treacherous enough as they were, pockmarked with potholes deep enough to swallow a tire, with sudden curves that could send cars skidding sideways into a ditch.

But in the ashen aftermath of Grandma Eleanor's forest fire, their perilous passage was practically impossible to perceive, with drifts of white and gray cinders blanketing the burnt landscape.

Silhouettes of blackened trees marched past the dusty silver sedan's grimy windows, the windscreen wipers fighting an unending battle against the snowing cinders. Charred wildlife and scorched debris crumbled beneath their wheels.

"Wonder if this car's got any music," Hayden Marsh stretched forward in the slanted front passenger seat to try the sedan's stereo.

"Do not approach the radio tower without calling ahead... I repeat – do not approach the radio tower without calling ahead... If there's anybody listening..."

"Fucking cocksucker," he punched the stereo, killing the broadcast of Braxton Shepherd's looped bait message.

Settling back into his seat, Hayden's face twisted with a pang of pain as Sterling wrestled the steering wheel around a sharp bend.

"Won't be too much longer before we shut him up for good," Riley promised, sitting behind Sterling in the backseat. Another sudden bend sent her sideways into Jesse's scrawny shoulder. With an annoyed grunt, she looked up at Sterling's reflection in the rearview mirror, "How much farther?"

"Depends on the road," he replied out of the side of his mouth, keeping his eyes fixed on the trail as they swerved around a fallen tree. "We should be there soon if we've got a clear run for the rest of the way though."

"Might be a good idea to stick around after the attack," Virge supposed behind Hayden, his rifle cradled in between his knees. "Let 'em see which way we hightail it outta town, see if they try chasing us back through the forest."

"Yeah, that could work," Riley agreed, leaning forward to glance sidelong at the grizzled war veteran. "If they run themselves off the road out here, there'll be even less men on hand to help guard Lake Springworth."

"And if they manage to make it through to the other side?" Jesse asked, turning his head as he sat in between the two, "What if they track us all the way back to the hangar?"

"We'll be waiting for 'em," Virge shrugged, fondly petting his rifle's barrel.

"Guys, if we can pull this off," Riley sat up in her seat as she began to realize, "We could probably hit the lake today."

"I think you're right," Hayden tried to look back at her, but his wound made him think twice about turning in his seat. "With all the shit we've been stirring up, I'm willing to bet they'd be down to a skeleton crew to watch over their camp."

Just the thought of being able to switch over from guerrilla warfare, to striking at the heart of Shepherd's operations, was enough to fill Riley's heart with hope.

She could picture the relief on her mother's face when they would surge through the trees, guns blazing out the windows, rescuing all of the women who had been captured over the past couple of weeks while massacring the men responsible.

"Count me in," Sterling nodded in anticipation as he straightened up the steering wheel. "First things first though."

The dusty silver sedan slowed to a roll as they broke through the blackened tree line, the modest town of Burview splaying out before them, with vast barren fields surrounding the ash-covered community.

Burview wasn't as big as Clementine, but it had been built up enough to encourage a cluster of small businesses to sprout up in the center of town.

Gravitating around the main intersection were a rundown roadhouse, a tapped-out gas station, a paint-peeled church and an ancient mechanic's garage, along with a looted collection of supply stores and hobby shops.

Standing on top of a hill on the far side of town was the radio tower, mindlessly emitting Shepherd's promise to welcome any survivors to his seemingly safe and civilized settlement.

"This place looks like it's been abandoned for years," Hayden craned his neck forward as they approached the outskirts of town.

"Don't believe everything you see," Sterling muttered, scanning the wide empty streets in the distance for a suitable location to stash the car.

Riley gazed out through her grimy window, seeing a dark smudge of a farmhouse presiding over an empty paddock in the distance. She flicked the window's switch for a better view, a thick film of ash sloughing down off the rolling glass pane.

Almost instantly, a noxious cloud of sulfur swept into the car.

"What the hell are you doing?" Virge spluttered, covering his mouth with one hand as he stretched across Jesse for the switch, lying just out of his reach, "Fucking close it!"

"Well, I guess we know what happened to all the guards," Hayden supposed with a pained cough as Riley shut the window again. He grimaced as he reached for the climate control, "They probably evacuated before the fire could –"

"Don't turn on the air-con," Jesse warned, knocking Hayden's arm off course before he could touch the controls. "You'll just suck more of the smoke in."

"I came here to snipe me some wife snatchers," Virge grumbled, giving his grab handle a dejected tug. "Don't tell me the bushfire's already smoked 'em out."

"They could still be hiding in some of the buildings," Sterling spoke over his shoulder as he peered through the windscreen at a nursery's greenhouse on the left.

"If they are, I doubt anyone's gonna notice us," Riley narrowed her eyes at every building they passed by. "The ash on the windows is too thick to see through. As long as we can keep it down out here until we're ready, I think we can still do some real damage."

"Starting to regret leaving the cognac back at the hangar," Jesse sighed before sitting forward with his hand on the back of Sterling's seat. He pointed towards a side street as they neared the town's main intersection, "Take us around the back of the mechanic's garage. Let's see if we can find a quiet way in."

They turned a corner, when a white panel van parked on the side of the road caught Sterling's attention.

"*Burview Electrical,*" he read the logo before pulling up alongside the work van. "Think that'll do the trick?"

"Oh, shit yeah," Jesse replied, leaning over Virge to squint through the grimy side window at the vehicle's murky silhouette. "Forget the garage – this is two birds, one stone."

Drawing their collars up over their noses, Riley, Sterling and Jesse climbed out of the sedan and stepped out onto the street, wisps of ash swirling around their shoes.

"Kill the engine and pop the hood," Jesse muttered to Riley before starting towards the white panel van.

"I'll cover the rear," Sterling whispered as he whipped out his pistol, following Jesse's lead.

Riley eased herself down into the driver's seat, shutting the door softly behind her.

"Are you sure he knows what he's doing?" Hayden asked anxiously as he watched Jesse break through the van's driver's side window. "I mean, how the hell does he even know how to hot-wire a car?"

"Relax," Riley gave him half a smile as she switched off the sedan's engine and tugged the hood's lever. "He might be a complete fucking idiot, but if there's one thing I can trust Jesse with, it's cars."

"I just hope he doesn't plan on driving the damn thing," Virge grunted from the backseat as Jesse climbed inside the work van. "Kid drinks like a man dying of thirst."

"Not like we have much of a choice," Hayden supposed with a begrudging sigh, "I can't turn a steering wheel, you can't work the pedals, and if we lose Sterling, we're fucked on the way back to the hangar." He turned to face Riley, "And I'm not letting you crash that van into the radio tower either."

Their plan was to knock Shepherd's looped broadcast off the air, taking out the antenna so that any other survivors wouldn't be lured into inadvertently inviting death and destruction to their door.

"How sweet," the words soured on her tongue, "You thinking I need your permission." She eyed Jesse emerging from the work van with a pair of jumper cables. As much as she wanted to be the one to ram the radio tower now – just to spite Hayden – she added, "I'm sure they'll come up with something."

They watched as Jesse ducked underneath the van's hood.

"I heard about what you said last night," Hayden reached up to focus the rearview mirror on Virge, "You wanting to *end my suffering*."

"Here we go," the old man grumbled, having anticipated the inevitable accusation. "Fine, I admit it. I was wrong. Happy?"

"You could lose the attitude," Hayden replied, still staring up at his reflection.

"Fucking kids these days," Virge muttered under his breath. "You know something, back when I was your age, I was watching men – *real men* – bleed out in the field on the regular. Medics gave 'em one look, a shot of morphine, and hopped on over to the next son of a bitch who was sorry for signing up."

"And thank you for your service," Hayden forced a measure of gratitude into his tone, before asking, "But were any of your army buddies ever mauled by a fucking mountain li–"

"Can you two cut the shit already?" Riley broke in, watching as Jesse crossed over to the sedan with the pair of jumper cables. "Virge, just apologize so we can get back to work."

"I'll pour a drink for Hayden and his feelings when all this is done," the grizzled war veteran offered. "As for an apology,

173

the two of you can both go fuck yourselves with a bucket of ice."

"Asshole," she exhaled in exasperation.

Staring at her shadowy reflection in the grimy side window, Riley couldn't help but start chuckling to herself, trying to imagine the mechanics of the old man's suggestion.

Hayden caught on the moment she glanced sidelong at him, quietly shaking in his seat, afraid that his wound would reopen if he cracked up.

Seeing the pair struggling to hold themselves together, Virge snorted aloud, his baritone laughter soon filling the car as they both gave in.

Two knocks on the sedan's front quarter panel brought the three of them back to their senses again, with Jesse retreating to a safe distance from the pair of jumper cables hooked up between the two vehicles, waiting expectantly with his eyes on Riley.

Sighing at the all too brief moment of relief, Riley refocused her attention back on the task at hand, clumsily fumbling for the keys with her bandaged fingers. Switching on the ignition, the sedan's engine revved, breathing new life into the white panel van's car battery.

Jesse flashed them a thumbs-up before ambling around to the other side of the van, reappearing in the side window's ashy obscurity as he climbed up into the work van's passenger seat, ducking his head underneath the dashboard.

Riley had no idea whether they wanted her to drive behind the van to the radio tower, but she began checking her mirrors all the same – with the sedan's hood flipped up, there wasn't much else to look at.

It was a fruitless exercise though.

The side mirrors were just as grimy as the windows, making it impossible to see.

"Cover your mouths for a second," she turned to Hayden and Virge, drawing her collar up over her nose with one hand while the other rested on the door handle. "I'm just gonna go clean the ash off the –"

CRACK!

Barks of gunfire erupted from the rear, squeezing off in rapid succession.

"Shit!" Riley shouted, hunching over the steering wheel as she clawed for the pistol tucked in the waistband of her jeans at the small of her back.

"Granger, get your ass back in here!!" Virge bellowed, shoving his door open and pointing his rifle out into the street.

The burst of bullets ceased just as suddenly as it had started, and an instant later, a driverless pickup truck bulled into the back of the white panel van, the pair of jumper cables slingshotting back into the sedan's windscreen.

"Riley, get us outta here!" Hayden yelled in between shallow breaths, shielding his wound with both hands.

"What about Jesse and Sterling!?" she stared back at his panicked eyes in disbelief.

"We'll come back for them," he insisted, sinking into his seat.

"Let go of my fucking – fuck!!" Virge roared in the backseat as he fought off a pair of hands wrestling for his rifle.

Before Riley could even flick the safety lever off her pistol, another attacker threw her door out wide and thrust the barrel of a revolver into her collarbone.

"Make a move and they all die," a gruff-voiced raider warned.

She could barely begin to turn her head before a heavy fist clocked her across the jaw.

175

CHAPTER 30

"Elroy to base, come in," a gruff voice floated through the darkness.

Riley Armstrong felt the cold rush of autumn wind on the side of her throbbing face.

Slowly stirring awake, she began to feel a dull ache in the back of her neck that seemed to sharpen with every bleary-eyed blink.

A bump in the road slammed the base of her skull against a metal railing, and she shot upright, her pupils dilating the moment she realized where she was – sitting inside the back of Braxton Shepherd's livestock truck, hurtling down the highway.

To her left were Hayden and Jesse.

To her right were Sterling and Virge.

All four of them were unconscious.

She tried to elbow Sterling, but she couldn't reach him.

Her bandaged hands were bound behind her back, the restraints looped around a railing for good measure.

Riley looked around for something to cut the cord with, when she caught sight of a pair of raiders sitting in between a cluster of wooden crates at the far end of the livestock container, using the truck's cabin as a windbreak.

They were the same two men who had tried to yank her back in through the second-story bedroom window of her grandmother's house.

"I say again – Elroy to base, come in," the gruff-voiced raider thumbed a walkie, his patience running thin.

The bald man unzipped his camouflage jacket as he stared up at the truck's ceiling, revealing an angry red rash where Riley had torn a clump of his beard from his neck and chin.

"You think they're part of a bigger group?" his nasally-voiced companion asked, wearing a hunting vest with a thick bandage wrapped across his broken nose. "It'd make sense. I mean – an attack on the supply run and another one in Burview on the same day? Maybe they've got some people hitting the lake right now."

"If *these guys* are part of a bigger group, our group's bigger," Elroy replied, before casting an uncertain glance at the radio in his hand. He lifted it up to his mouth again, "Base, fucking answer!"

"Elroy, you're on the wrong channel," Braxton Shepherd's voice crackled through from the other side. "Didn't ya get the message? Those raiders who set up the ambush yesterday might be listening in."

"Good, let them listen to this," Elroy threw a triumphant glance over at their new prisoners, "We just caught a couple of armed trespassers near the radio tower. Four men and a woman. Figured maybe we could use them for leverage over anyone else they might be working with."

"Nice work, guys," Shepherd replied, holding a brief in-audible conversation with someone on the other end before speaking clearly through the walkie again, "Doc Quinn wants to have a look at them. I'm gonna send Jimmy's team on over to stand in for ya. You've earned the rest of the day off. Come on home."

"Already halfway there," the broken-nosed raider grimaced as he tried to snort. He snatched up his hunting rifle as he caught Riley eyeing them both, "Looks like we got an early bird."

"I was hoping she'd wake up before we got back," Elroy remarked as he lurched to his feet, grabbing the container's roof beams to steady himself against the truck's rocking as he made his way towards their captives. He loomed over her, "You and your friends killed a lot of good men yesterday, you know that?"

"They must not have been very *good* then," Riley glared up at him with hate in her eyes.

He was the same man who had shared a smile with her in passing, minutes before he had executed Grandma Eleanor in front of her own home.

"You cocky little bitch!" the nasally-voiced raider shouted as he clambered upright, slinging his hunting rifle over his shoulder.

"That voice sounds familiar," Elroy grunted, bracing his legs as the truck took a turn. "You were the one who lured our boys over to that truck stop yesterday... You and your two sisters, my ass," he looked over the four bound men before nodding towards his approaching companion. "Halsey's brother was on that crew. Haven't heard from them since. Burned to death in that fire, probably."

Riley knew that she wouldn't be able to escape the raiders' reprisal.

Not with her bandaged hands tied behind her back.

Kicking was out too.

The ache of her strained groin rendered her legs almost completely useless.

Whatever they had in store for her, there wasn't a damn thing she could do about it.

But she wasn't going to beg either.

"Fuck Halsey," Riley spat, sneering up at the broken-nosed man. "And fuck your brother too. You attacked us first, and now you wanna cry about it because we hit you back? Pathetic pieces of shit."

"Fuck my brother, huh?" Halsey clenched his jaw before dropping to one knee. Jerking the stock of his hunting rifle up to his shoulder, he swept the barrel from side to side over the row of prisoners. "Alright, fuck your boyfriend then. Elroy, which one of these fuckers do you think would be desperate enough to stick his dick into this bitch?"

"I recognize this one from yesterday," Elroy pointed out Hayden. "He was already gone by the time that blonde started screaming though. Don't think he's boyfriend material."

"Maybe this skinny runt then," Halsey lined up his sights on Jesse instead, one eye on Riley as he toyed with the trigger.

She simply stared back at him.

Riley knew that her friends were already as good as dead.

The raiders were only interested in taking the women. They killed all of the men.

But she also knew that the slightest facial twitch could get one of them killed a whole lot sooner, and there was still a chance that they could do some damage together when they reached Lake Springworth.

She just had to keep the raiders' attention focused on her

until an opportunity presented itself.

"Or maybe she likes them older," Halsey judged from her lack of reaction, turning his gun on Sterling next. He glanced back at her again, snarling in frustration before switching over to Virge, "Or how about I just start with Grandpa and work my fucking way down!?"

"Enough!" Elroy shouted, swatting the rifle's barrel up at the ceiling. He zipped up his camouflage jacket against the wind as the other prisoners began to stir, "Listen, we do what Shepherd says, and we've got the rest of the day off. All we gotta do is bring them back to the lodge, and they're somebody else's problem."

"No, we'll still be your problem," Sterling Granger struggled against his restraints, staring daggers at the two men. "Because when I get outta here, I'm gonna kill every last one of you miserable fucking bastards. You better pray my wife's okay, or I'll grind your bones into dust while you're still screaming."

"Whoever she is, I'm sure she's fine," Elroy grinned back, his scarred skin stretching tight over his rash-ridden chin. With a wink, he added, "She's probably even enjoying herself."

"YOU MOTHERFUCKER!! I SWEAR I'LL –"

Halsey silenced Sterling with a rifle butt to his sternum.

With all the wind knocked out of him, Granger keeled over to one side, hacking and wheezing and glowering up at them with murderous intent.

"You're a big tough guy, huh?" Virge goaded the broken-nosed raider. "Does that make you feel strong, beating up a prisoner with his hands tied behind his back?"

"Shut up," Halsey warned, menacing in his nasal voice.

He's gonna get himself killed, Riley looked past Sterling to furrow her eyebrows at Virge, wondering what the hell he was thinking. Neither one of them was making her job of keeping the spotlight focused on her any easier.

As if Virge could hear Riley's thoughts, the grizzled war veteran locked eyes with her, before pointedly glancing towards Halsey's hunting rifle.

The broken-nosed raider was cradling his weapon in both hands as he paced up and down the row of captives, relying on his footing alone to contend with the livestock container's swaying as the truck roared down the highway.

"Why stop there?" Virge continued, his dog tags jingling as he leaned forward defiantly. "Why not beat up an old man too, while you're at it?"

"Oh no, don't hurt Grandpa," Elroy pleaded sarcastically as he held onto one of the container's roof beams. He shrugged at Virge without a shred of pity, "I took you outta the crosshairs once already, old man, my good deed's done for the day."

The bald raider chuckled to himself as he turned a blind eye, too preoccupied with the passing landscape to notice Jesse's shoes slowly snaking towards his boots.

"I guess you can't really blame the poor guy," Riley supposed, drawing Halsey's attention as he drew up alongside her. "He just wants everyone to treat him like he's a real man again."

"Yeah, you got that right," the nasally-voiced raider narrowed his eyes at Virge, "Legless fucker needs to learn how to keep his damn mouth shut."

"Oh, I wasn't talking about him," she smirked up at Halsey. "Must've felt pretty humiliating yesterday, right? Having your nose broken by a girl."

"Fuck you!!" Halsey finally broke, whirling on her with his boot raised.

With a surge of icy adrenaline, Riley seized the opportunity they had been waiting for.

Summoning what little strength she had left in her throbbing thighs, she drew up her knees and flailed out with both feet at his supporting leg, kicking her heels into his shin.

Halsey buckled, losing his balance in the back of the truck.

He toppled over, with his weapon clattering to the floor.

Sterling – still lying breathless on his side – caught the hunting rifle's stock with his boot, sliding the firearm in a wide arc across the floor towards Virge's hip.

"Gonna stop you right there," Elroy cautioned them with a no-nonsense tone, still on his feet.

The raider's revolver was leveled at the older pair of prisoners, having caught them in his sights just before Sterling could kick the rifle butt into Virge's bound hands.

Wondering how the bald man was still standing, Riley glanced sidelong at the tangle of bodies on her left.

Jesse – using both of his feet in a fit of desperation – was frantically shoving Halsey backwards, sending the man careening over to the other side of the container.

Riley's pupils dilated in dread at the sight of blood on the raider's hunting vest.

She slowly turned her head to the side, seeing splotches of red glistening in between the folds of Hayden's puffy black jacket.

Her heart dropped in her chest the moment she realized what she had done.

After tripping up the raider, Halsey had fallen into Hayden, ripping his stitches and reopening the wound.

Despite her best efforts, she had gotten the wrong man killed.

Working his jaw, Hayden Marsh met her gaze with wide

fearful eyes, gaping at her in wordless agony.

CHAPTER 31

They sat in somber silence as hues of yellow and gold swam past the bars of the livestock truck, the autumn forest surrounding Lake Springworth untouched by the blaze of Grandma Eleanor's bushfire.

Occasionally, a break in the trees would give way to a wooden guard tower, with the sentries manning each post waving them on up the narrow winding road.

Still sitting with her hands tied behind her back, Riley Armstrong stared down at Hayden Marsh's lifeless body as it bounced alongside her.

As a precaution, Elroy and Halsey had kept his corpse bound to the container's railing, but at least they had been gracious enough to cover him up with a blanket from one of the wooden crates behind the truck's cabin.

Riley was still unsure of how she felt about the former college footballer's death.

She had only known him for the past three months, but after having lived in such close proximity at her grandmother's house, seeing each other at every meal and going on supply runs to Clementine together, it certainly felt like she had known him for a lot longer.

And not that she had ever cared to admit it – but between him, Jesse and Greg – Hayden had been the most tolerable of the three.

He had also been the biggest coward.

During the attack on Grandma Eleanor's farm, he had hidden down in the wine cellar while everyone else was either getting killed or captured.

Riley had thought that she could sympathize with him last night, when he had expressed his regret over his absence – but after they had been set upon from behind in Burview, and his first instinct had been to leave Jesse and Sterling behind – she knew what type of man he really was.

She found that it was easier to deal with his death if she hated him.

Rows of log cabins marched past as the livestock truck's big wheels slowed, and they soon swung around in a gravel cul-de-sac in front of a hulking wooden lodge.

Lake Springworth shimmered through the autumn leaves on the side of the big backcountry abode, with a handful of small fishing boats dotting the calm waters in the distance.

For a split second, it almost felt as though they had been sent to a summer camp in the middle of autumn. Any moment now, one of the camp counselors would come out to greet the new arrivals, assign each of them to a cabin, and for their first group activity, they could figure out what to do with Hayden's body before his family found out.

A metallic screech pealed across the settlement, shaking Riley back to her senses as the truck's ramp swung down with a heavy resonating *clang* on the ground.

"Well, my job's done, I'm outta here," Halsey decided, descending the ramp without a backwards glance, having had his fill of vengeance – intentional or otherwise.

"Prick," Elroy muttered under his breath as he held his revolver on the row of prisoners.

The livestock container rocked from side to side as a sudden wave of olive, khaki and brown climbed aboard, a group of armed men wearing camouflage jackets and fatigues filling the truck.

Half of the guards stooped to release the captives' restraints from the railings, making sure to keep their hands tied behind their backs, while the other half kept watch beside Elroy.

"On your feet, old man," one of the guards grunted, tugging Virge by the arm.

"If you can get my legs working again, I'll suck your dick," the grizzled war veteran snorted before scowling up at Elroy. "Tell me you ass-monkeys checked the trunk when you pulled us outta that sedan."

"We take people for everything they're worth," the bald man snorted, jerking his head towards the cluster of wooden crates at the far end of the livestock container. "Yeah, we checked."

"Better luck next time, asshole," Virge told the guard holding his arm as Elroy fished his wheelchair out from one of the crates.

Riley almost asked if they happened to have another chair as they hauled her upright. She was barely able to carry her own weight down the truck's ramp, begrudgingly having to lean on one of the guards for support as her strained groin grated in agony.

They spilled out into the gravel cul-de-sac.

The afternoon sun was still high in the sky, but daylight was already beginning to wane, struggling to shine through the bushfire's shroud of smoke still lingering in the air.

While they waited for Virge to join them, Riley gazed around at the settlement.

Aside from the armed guards escorting the prisoners and patrolling the perimeter, the log cabin community held a certain rustic appeal.

Neatly-swept piles of autumn leaves lined the gravel paths, while warm orange glows emanated from within the wooden walls and windows of the small cottages facing the cul-de-sac.

In a nearby clearing, a pair of sheltered van-sized diesel generators rumbled beside a big wood shed, contending with the engine of the idling livestock truck.

"Welcome to Lake Springworth!" the cheery voice of their camp counselor called over the noise from the truck.

Riley turned to see Braxton Shepherd, her head cocking at the sight of him wearing Nolan Armstrong's fur-lined leather aviator jacket as he came out to greet them.

He ambled down the hulking wooden lodge's front stairs, minding his step over his paunchy physique as he approached them with a wide smile and an outstretched hand.

She furrowed her eyebrows at him in disbelief, wondering how the man could so brazenly pretend that he hadn't dragged her mother into the back of the livestock truck just yesterday, moments before ordering Grandma Eleanor's execution.

Even now, he was wearing her father's jacket, stolen from Keith Bowman's corpse before the raiders had fled the scene.

"You're Riley, right?" Shepherd asked, beaming at her with his deep laugh lines. "I remember ya from yesterday. I sure am glad ya reconsidered our offer to join us!"

"*Offer?*" she echoed incredulously, "You fucking –"

"Braxton Shepherd, pleased to meet ya," he cut across her

outrage as he turned his attention towards Jesse, Sterling and Virge. His outstretched hand lingered in the air for an awkward moment before he glanced sidelong at Elroy, "Are those restraints really necessary?"

Jesse stared at Shepherd's friendly face in confusion.

Similarly, Virge frowned at the warmth in his voice, wondering how a neighborly man like Braxton had ever found himself in charge of a congregation of coldblooded killers.

"You gunned down my brother, you piece of shit!" Sterling roared, making a lunge for Shepherd, only to be stopped short by a pair of guards. "Where the fuck is my wife!? You take me to my Abbie, right now, or I'm gonna murder every last –"

One of the guards silenced him with a strip of duct tape.

"There's your answer," Elroy shrugged at Shepherd over the sound of Sterling's muffled death threats.

"I just feel like we're giving off the wrong impression," Braxton folded his arms over the top of his belly. He frowned slightly as he looked over the captives, "I thought you said there were *four* men?"

"One died on the way over," Elroy answered, jerking his head towards Hayden's body in the back of the livestock truck. "Blood loss. Real nasty scratch. From a cougar, they told me. Surprised he even walked away from something like that."

"That's a real shame," Shepherd shook his head with a heavy sigh. He studied the remaining prisoners with feigned sympathy, "I'm sorry for your loss. We need good strong men to help us hold this place together."

"Did I hear that right?" Jesse croaked with his dry throat, peering at the others for confirmation, each of them as equally as perplexed. He turned back towards Shepherd, "If you need good strong men, here's an idea – stop fucking killing them."

"Oh, ya got us all wrong, son," Braxton's sickening neighborly smile returned. "Like I told Riley yesterday, everybody's really dedicated to making this thing work, and ya know what they say – more hands means less work." He gave a conceding shrug as he continued, "Sure, we might run into a little trouble every now and then, with this group or that group, but we never fire first. There's enough room around here for anyone who's willing to earn their keep."

"That's bullshit," Riley seethed, seeing straight through the civil snake's bold-faced lies, "*Never fire first.* We saw what your people did in Clementine. You lined up all those men in front of the general store and you executed them. Then you came to my grandma's house and you gave the order to kill an old woman for trying to defend her family." She glared at Elroy with ice in her eyes, "You're dead for that, by the way. Might not be today. Might not be tomorrow. But I swear, one way or another, I'm gonna empty your fucking revolver into your fucking face."

"Okay, I think we got off on the wrong foot here," Braxton held up his hands, trying to soothe the situation somehow, as if he could salvage any semblance of civility after slaughtering their people.

"Why are we even standing here right now?" Jesse wondered, looking around at Riley, Sterling and Virge, surrounded by the guards gathered in the gravel cul-de-sac. "Everybody knows, you kill the men and take the women. Why keep the rest of us alive?"

"Yeah, can we get this shit over with already?" Virge grumbled in his chair. "I'm due for a piss right about now, and if I'm doing it out here in front of everybody, I'd rather have the bullet first."

"How about this," Shepherd offered him a disarming smile, "I'll ask Elroy here to wheel ya out back so the two of ya can take care of business. The rest of us – we'll head inside, and I'll explain everything."

"What's there to explain?" Riley's question fell on deaf ears as Braxton turned his back on them all, leading the way up the hulking wooden lodge's front stairs. "What could you possibly say that could justify the shit you've done?"

Curious at the invitation, and with nothing left to lose except for his life that was already as good as gone, Jesse was the first to follow him up the steps.

"Fuck it," Virge shrugged, utterly immobile with his hands tied as he glowered at Elroy. "Not like I have much of a choice anyway."

Still restrained between a pair of guards, Sterling's protests were muffled by his gag as Elroy took hold of the grizzled war veteran's wheelchair.

Riley glanced sidelong at Granger, wondering what he was getting so worked up over. Admittedly, Shepherd's suggestion had been strange, to say the least, but surprisingly more reasonable than they ever could have hoped for.

Even she was willing to follow the glib-tongued son of a bitch back inside the lodge, if only to hear his explanation before she could come up with a way to kill him.

Despite his hands being bound behind his back, Sterling managed to wrestle one man to the ground before another pair of guards grabbed his forearms from behind.

Together, the four raiders dragged him across the gravel cul-de-sac and forced him up the lodge's steps.

Watching the intensity of Sterling's struggle, Riley didn't catch on until after Virge and Elroy had already disappeared around the corner of the big backcountry abode.

That's how they get you, Granger's voice echoed in her ears. *They pretend they're your friends, and then they kill all the men, and take all the women.*

Riley's heart plunged into her stomach.

Shepherd had been playing them all along.

He was doing what he did best – luring them into a false sense of security until they followed him like a flock of sheep.

And in Riley's condition, a firm tug on her arm was all that it took to get her aching legs moving again.

She stared up at the hulking wooden lodge, with its double doors thrown wide open, like the predatory jaws of a monstrous maw, ready to snap shut on a new chunk of fresh meat.

CHAPTER 32

Riley Armstrong kept glancing over her shoulder, expecting – hoping – to see Virge, free of his bonds, wheeling himself around the front of the lodge with Elroy's revolver in hand, ready to rain hellfire down on the raiders responsible for killing and kidnapping all of the innocent people who had unknowingly invited the wolves to their door.

She was still staring over her shoulder when she stumbled on the threshold of the big backcountry abode, reigniting the flames of her throbbing thigh muscles once again.

Gritting her teeth against the pain, she gazed around at the lodge's interior.

Her jaw would have dropped if she hadn't been clenching it so tightly.

Flanked by the guards as she stood awestruck in the entrance, it felt as though Shepherd's foreboding wooden lodge had transformed into the foyer of a lofty ski resort, with its seasonal staff arriving early in the last few weeks of autumn to gear up for the peak holiday period.

On one side of the foyer, a towering chimney rose up through the vaulted second-story ceiling. A large stone fireplace bathed the room with its warm golden glow, its crackling flames exhaling a crispy sweet aroma, imbuing the inviting scent into the sprawling leather armchairs arranged around the hearth.

Beside a staircase that led to the upper level, a row of floor-to-ceiling windows along the back wall offered a beautiful view of Lake Springworth's peaceful waters, framed by picturesque autumn forests and mountain peaks in the distance.

Despite the danger they were in, Riley could feel her tide of anxiety ebbing away.

"Well, here we are," Braxton Shepherd turned around with a broad grin on his face. "Suddenly the end of the world doesn't seem so bad, right? We've got electricity from the generators, running water, plenty of food –"

"Got anything to drink?" Jesse croaked, scouring the room for signs of a bar.

"Unfortunately, no," Shepherd replied with a slight slump in his shoulders. "I wish I had a couple beers around here for ya, but you'd have to line up behind everyone else first."

Most of the guards chuckled, but a few of them swallowed their thirst with hard-eyed stares.

"You said you were gonna explain everything," Riley prompted him, having recovered from the spell of their stunning surroundings. "Why the hell did you bring us here?"

"That's a good question," although Braxton dodged giving it an answer, "Before we go down that road though, could we…" He motioned for one of his men to remove the strip of duct tape from Sterling's mouth. Shepherd offered a smile of apology as the gag ripped free, "You're probably not gonna listen to anything we have to say until ya see your wife, right?"

"I wouldn't be so sure," Sterling glared back at him, unbridled fury broiling in the shadows of his dark eyes. "I could stand to listen to your screams for a good long while, until you tell me where to find my Abbie."

"Message received, loud and clear!" Braxton held up his hands in surrender, before a thin line creased his brow. "We've got an Abbie Granger here – I only remember the name because she's got something wrong with her thyroid. Is that the woman you're looking for?"

"Yeah, that's her," Sterling's rage instantly evaporated, his pupils dilating with concern. "Has she been getting her meds?"

"Ya can ask her for yourself," Shepherd nodded towards the staircase leading up to the second level. "We put her up in one of the lakeside rooms. Boys, mind taking our new friend here to see his wife?"

With his hands still tied behind his back, Granger allowed four of Shepherd's men to escort him towards the stairs.

"Wait!" Riley blurted out, locking eyes with Sterling as he mounted the first step. She glanced at Braxton – the same person responsible for the Clementine massacre and the shootout at her grandmother's farm – disguised as a neighborly man with a friendly smile, "Can't you see he's just trying to separate us? There's no guarantee that your wife was ever here. What if they've already killed Virge, and you're next?"

Shepherd sighed wearily at the accusation.

"He knows about her thyroid," Sterling reasoned in a hollow voice, although he avoided her gaze just as much as he was avoiding the probable truth. He tilted his head down at the staircase's handrail, mulling it over before summoning his resolve, "If there's even a chance of me seeing my wife again... I'll take it."

He sized up the four guards flanking him, and after one final moment of hesitation, he began marching up the stairs, like a man marching to his death.

Riley glanced sidelong at Jesse as the five men reached the upper level and disappeared around a corner.

With Hayden, Virge and Sterling gone, it was just down to the two of them now.

"If I'm being honest," Jesse looked around the room at Shepherd's remaining guards, "I thought I was gonna die back in Burview – so you can imagine my surprise when I woke up in the back of that truck." He glanced at Braxton, "We can't really blame your men for what happened to Hayden either, so I'm just gonna be optimistic here and say, as long as you don't kill me, that's probably a good sign." He chuckled to himself as he turned towards Riley, "Just don't run off on me looking for your mom."

"No, I think the rest of us can stick together now," Shepherd chortled, happy to dispel the tension in the room. He turned towards a corridor on the left, "Well, looks like we owe ya some answers about this place. That guy, Granger's gonna hear it from his wife, and Elroy's probably telling – Virge, was it? But the two of ya are gonna get it straight from the Doc. Come on, this way."

With their hands bound behind their backs, Riley and Jesse didn't have any other choice but to follow Shepherd as he led them down the corridor, the wooden interior of the passage soon giving way to whitewashed drywall.

"What the fuck?" Riley had to glance back over her shoulder, just to make sure that they were still in the same building.

If the last room had been reminiscent of a ski resort, then they had just entered the lodge's very own private hospital ward.

Men and women wearing scrubs paced around the cavernous room's vinyl flooring, checking clipboards against high-tech medical equipment and scribbling notes. Each monitoring device flashed with an array of ever-changing vitals, hooked up to a spider web of cables that branched out to several observation rooms.

There were six pairs of doors and windows lining the lab's walls, marked with 'A' through to 'F'. Curtains were drawn across each of the windows.

One of the nurses emerged from the door marked with 'D', bringing his clipboard over to a desk set in between two medicine cabinets at the back of the lab.

"Room D's ready," the nurse reported, sharing his work with a refined blonde woman wearing a white lab coat.

"Good," she replied, handing him back the clipboard. She adjusted her glasses as she glanced up at the new arrivals, before adding, "Send in the next appointment."

Riley stared around in confusion, wondering what the hell was going on.

This was the last place that she would have expected to find a hospital.

They must be running some kind of experiment, she quickly concluded. *Why else would they have a setup like this in the middle of nowhere?*

Riley's heart froze in her chest as she imagined her mother in one of the rooms, requiring round-the-clock medical attention after enduring the sick and twisted depravities that Shepherd's men had subjected her to.

An angry tear trickled down her grimy cheek as she pushed the thought out of her mind.

Following the blonde woman's orders, the nurse obediently crossed the room and hunched over a desk. He traced his forefinger down the side of a chart and tapped one of the entries before speaking into a microphone.

"Number forty-seven," his voice called over the intercom, "Report to the lab, please. Number forty-seven."

The woman in the lab coat rose from her desk to greet the newcomers, checking a clock on the wall as her shoes squeaked over the vinyl floor.

"Good afternoon," she studied Riley before turning to the guards with a dismissive hand wave. "You can leave now – you're crowding the room and we need space in here to work."

"Thanks for your help, boys," Braxton bade his men a warmer farewell, "We'll call ya over the intercom if we need ya to come on back."

A few of the guards grumbled among themselves, but they filed out of the lab all the same.

"My name is Doctor Alyssa Quinn," the blonde woman introduced herself before gesturing towards a pair of black leather office chairs, "Why don't you both sit down?"

Almost involuntarily, Riley slumped into the nearest seat, her strained groin grateful for the reprieve.

"I'd prefer to stand," Jesse replied as he dawdled around the room, taking a withdrawn interest in some of the medical equipment. "I think I sat wrong for most of the ride on the way over here. My back's killing me."

"Wait until you're my age, son," Braxton chuckled as he eased himself into the second chair instead. He swiveled his seat towards the doctor, "Riley, here, was with that group we brought in yesterday. Not sure where the rest of her friends came from, but we've been having trouble ever since. Lost one

197

team in the bushfire, and another on the way to the chicken coop. Might've lost more if Elroy's boys didn't pick them up in Burview."

"So tell me, Riley," Quinn began, sitting on a nearby table with one leg crossed over the other, both of her hands clasped in her lap, "Why have you been interfering with our operations?"

"Well, Alyssa," Shepherd interjected, glancing at Riley with a sheepish grin, "I think we should start off by telling them what we're doing here. Maybe if they understood wh–"

Quinn silenced him with a hand, her question lingering in the air.

"You attacked us first," Riley answered flatly, already beginning to hate the refined blonde woman.

"So this is retaliation, then," Alyssa supposed, stifling a smirk. "Did the two of you really believe that you could go blow for blow against us and succeed?"

"Oh, there's a whole lot more than just the *four* of us," Riley fired back, keenly aware that even now, she and Jesse were almost certainly the only two left alive, and she was barely in any condition to fight. She could only hope that they wouldn't call her bluff, "If you think that just a handful of us were behind all of those attacks, then you're in for a hell of a fight when the main force gets here."

"I knew they had to be part of a bigger group," Braxton took the bait easier than Riley had expected. He leaned towards her with his neighborly smile, "Is all this violence really necessary though? Maybe ya could radio your friends and bring them on over. I'm sure there's a way we can put everything behind us without any more bloodshed."

"Cut the shit, Shepherd," she spat before turning her icy glare on Quinn. Trying her luck with her newfound leverage, she made her demands, "Let my mom go. Let all of the women go. And maybe, *maybe*, we won't come back here and kill every last one of you." She shot a glance at the nurses who had stopped to listen in, "That goes for the rest of you too. You think we give a fuck about whether you're holding a gun or a pen after everything that's been taken from us?"

"Yeah, she doesn't mess around," Jesse backed her up from behind a desk. "There was this one guy who was unarmed, on his knees, begging for mercy, and she still blew his brains out at point blank range." He peered over the top of a computer screen at Quinn, "You know, come to think about it, he was a doctor too."

"Is that so?" Alyssa adjusted her glasses as she studied Riley again. "I could use more people like you. Not afraid to do whatever is necessary, however morally ambiguous." She turned her head to the side, but kept her gaze on Riley, "Nurse, bring me the register."

One of her assistants picked up a clipboard and hugged it to her chest, taking a wide berth around Jesse before delivering the register to Doctor Quinn.

For once, Riley was grateful that her hands were tied behind her back, because she had a profound urge to rub the back of her clammy neck. It seemed that both Shepherd and Quinn had bought her story of a larger group gearing up to take revenge against the raiders.

We might be able to walk outta here alive, Riley began thinking to herself.

All she had to do now was maintain her poker face.

The whole room watched with bated breaths as the doctor flipped through the charts on the clipboard. She ran her finger down the last page before smirking to herself.

"I'll let each of you choose one person to leave with you," Quinn decided, handing the register back to the nurse. "But whether they choose to leave is entirely up to them."

"What the hell does that mean?" Riley furrowed her eyebrows, her confusion darting between Alyssa and Braxton.

"Doctor Quinn?" a familiar voice called from behind. "I'm here for my appointment."

Riley spun around to see Aunt Lorraine, unrestrained and unescorted, with a broad smile across her face.

CHAPTER 33

"Riley!?" Lorraine Tipton stood at the lab's entrance, the matronly woman's beady eyes positively beaming behind her thick glasses, "I'm so happy you finally made it. Susan's gonna be thrilled when she finds out you're here!"

"What the hell?" Riley frowned over at Jesse as if she had missed something. She turned back to her aunt, "Where's Mom?"

"She's upstairs," Lorraine replied as she gave Shepherd a little wave. "We're roomies now, can you believe it? Oh, Riley, you're gonna love it here!"

"Yeah, about that…" she faltered, thrown off by her aunt's enthusiasm. "I'm not staying. We came here to rescue you."

One of the male nurses cleared his throat, standing beside the door to the observation room marked 'D', impatiently tapping his pen against his clipboard.

"Oh, my silly little niece, you haven't finished the tour yet," Lorraine shook her head with an amused grin before crossing over to the nurse. She twirled a lock of her greasy brown hair, "Is there any chance Room F is ready?"

"I'd say another hour before we're good to go," the nurse

assigned to Room F reported.

"That's longer than I'm willing to wait," Lorraine's cheeks were already flushing with anticipation. She breathed a heavy sigh before opening the door to Room D, "Well, I haven't tried this one before."

"What the fuck are you giving her?" Riley shot an accusing glare at Doctor Quinn as Lorraine disappeared inside the observation room. "What the hell is this place?"

"I'll take it from here, Doc," Shepherd wheeled his office chair over to the desk where Alyssa was sitting, turning back to face Riley and Jesse together. "Remember the asteroid that hit us a couple months ago? As if ya could forget, right? Well, we've known it was coming for years – decades, actually."

"Okay," Riley furrowed her eyebrows, "What does that have to do with anything?"

"Oh, just about everything," Shepherd shared a sidelong smile with Quinn. "Alyssa's dad knew the world wasn't gonna be prepared for the day of The Fall. I mean, ya saw those nukes, they completely missed the mark! That's why we – and a whole lot of good people – took it on ourselves to set this place up, and I gotta tell ya, I sure am glad we did."

"Hey, you remember yesterday in the truck stop," Jesse looked over at Riley as he leaned against a desk in the next aisle of workstations. "Didn't Sterling say this place was meant to be some kinda cult community?"

"Only small minds talk in rumors," Alyssa crossed her arms, the blonde doctor's touch of refinement souring. "Not everyone believed in my father and what we were doing, but that didn't matter. There were enough of us who did. And there are plenty more who have come back these past few months."

"Your dad would be proud if he was still here," Braxton spoke softly in his warm neighborly tone as he leaned towards Quinn. "We're gonna save a lot of people with this place."

"Are you fucking hearing yourselves!?" Riley couldn't keep herself quiet any longer. "You've murdered innocent people by the dozen. There were groups and communities that were doing just fine until you came along. You've killed a hell of a lot more people than you've saved!"

"We're talking about the survival of the entire human race!" Alyssa fired back, her eyes seething behind her glasses. "You don't know anything about that asteroid, but my father did. He knew that it would come. He knew that there was nothing our government could do to stop it. And he knew exactly what we'd have to do in order to survive what came next. The sacrifices we've had to make, the lines we've crossed…"

"It's okay, Alyssa," Shepherd patted her arm gently, before swiveling his seat to look back at the nurses who had stopped to listen in. "With everything we're doing, sometimes it feels like we've got the weight of the world on our shoulders. We knew this wouldn't be easy, but we're making it happen anyway. We've just gotta keep the wheels turning until we get to where we're going."

"I've dedicated my life's work to this place," Quinn muttered under her breath as the medical staff returned to work. "The least they could do is try to understand why."

"Okay, let's pretend we actually give a shit about what you're doing," Jesse shrugged, overcome by his curiosity. "What does a hospital-lodge beside a lake in the middle of nowhere have to do with the survival of the human race? I mean, I hate to break it to you, but the asteroid's already landed – and guess what? We're still alive."

Braxton opened his mouth to explain, when the door to Room D opened again, and Aunt Lorraine emerged with ruffled hair and a glad smile.

"Well, that didn't take as long as I was hoping," Lorraine bit her pinkie's fingernail as she turned to gaze back inside the room. "I'm not sure whether to be disappointed or to take it as a compliment."

"Either way, thank you for your time," the male nurse standing beside the door gave her a polite smile before slipping inside.

"I think I'm gonna take a shower," Lorraine mentioned in passing to the nurse assigned to Room F, "Would you mind calling me back down when this one's ready?"

Sick of not getting a straight answer, Riley was determined to at least find out what was in the observation rooms.

She clambered to her feet, gritting her teeth against the wave of pain from her strained groin.

"Let her see for herself," Shepherd waved off the edgy medical staff standing by.

Staggering, Riley ventured closer to Room D's open door, peering past the half-drawn privacy curtain to see the male nurse hunching over a hospital bed.

A pair of handcuffs rattled softly against the bed frame as Riley entered the room, and a shirtless black man with a well-built physique came into view, crying silent tears as he stared catatonically up at the ceiling.

Drawing the patient's blanket up over his waist, the nurse noticed Riley's presence in the corner of his eye. Whirling around, he knocked the IV pole aside in his haste to usher her back out.

"He's doing his part for humanity," the nurse tried to offer some semblance of an explanation while closing the door. "He just needs some more time to get used to the idea."

CHAPTER 34

Riley Armstrong stared in stunned silence at the closed observation room's door, trying to process what she had just seen, when Virge Norton's baritone blustering interrupted her thoughts.

"I can wheel myself in, you fucking ass-monkey!" he growled at Elroy's attempts to push his wheelchair.

"You cut his restraints?" Doctor Quinn eyed the third newcomer's free hands as the pair of men entered the room.

"It was either that or unzip his pants myself," Elroy answered brusquely. The bald raider in the camouflage jacket looked over at Shepherd, "You said I could have the rest of the day off. Can I go now?"

"Maybe ya can hang around for a little while longer," Braxton replied, glancing pointedly at Riley standing beside Room D, "At least until we can bring everybody up to speed."

"Fucking Halsey..." Elroy muttered under his breath.

"Well, this is an even bigger shithole than I expected," Virge remarked, staring around at the hospital ward's medical equipment. "Nice big house next to a nice big lake, and not a single fucking bottle of whiskey in sight!"

206

"I knew something was off about this place," Jesse agreed, still leaning back against a desk as he tried to catch Riley's attention.

She locked eyes with him from across the room, her gaze dropping to his hip, where a glint of metal flashed from in between his bound hands.

"Take what we need, leave what we don't," Shepherd folded his arms over his paunchy belly with a sheepish shrug, "As much as I love a good whiskey, we don't need hangovers around here. Everybody's gotta make a sacrifice."

"Is that why you've got that man chained up in there?" Riley finally found her voice as she stepped away from Room D. "Is his freedom another sacrifice? What do you *need* from a guy who's handcuffed to a hospital bed?"

"Hold on, where the fuck's Granger?" Virge suddenly realized, sitting up in his chair to look over the tops of workstations and computer screens.

"Upstairs with his wife, apparently," Jesse answered skeptically, nodding towards Shepherd, "At least according to *him*. All I saw was four armed thugs escorting a prisoner."

Riley glanced around at the other observation rooms, realizing that there were probably five more men who were as equally as incapacitated as the shirtless man she had just seen. For all they knew, Sterling might be the next patient to occupy a hospital bed.

"What kinda fucking operation are you running here!?" she glowered at Alyssa.

"Exactly that – a *fucking operation*," Quinn quipped, stifling a smirk. "My father predicted that we'd lose countless lives when that asteroid hit, both immediately upon impact, and in the chaos that followed." She glanced sidelong at

Shepherd, drawing strength from his encouraging smile before continuing, "So we built this birth center to ensure that we could bring up a new generation of people in an efficient and controlled manner when the time came. And evidently, that time is now."

"It's been three fucking months, you crazy bitch!" Riley shouted, sick to her stomach. "Sure, people have died, but the world hasn't ended. That asteroid didn't kill off the rest of the human race. You don't have to force people to repopulate the planet!!"

"I knew I shouldn't have expected you to understand," Alyssa waved her hand dismissively, closing herself off from the conversation.

"Is that what's going on here?" Virge raised his eyebrows in disbelief, his dog tags jingling as he looked around at the nurses in the room. "This whole time, we thought you were just a gang of raiders and wife snatchers. That would actually make sense. Now you're saying we've been killing a bunch of misled dickheads who thought they were saving the world?" He snorted in amusement, "Well, either way, I can't say anyone's gonna miss 'em."

"I don't mean to kink shame," Jesse frowned, his scrawny arms subtly flexing behind his back. "But if you've got *men* in those rooms, and you've told them that their job is to repopulate the planet, why the hell would they need to be handcuffed?"

"I can answer that one," Braxton smiled sidelong at Doctor Quinn before leaning forward in his chair. "They aren't exactly volunteers. It was Alyssa's dad who laid down the law when we first started building this place. Just like the *no alcohol* rule, anyone who joined us willingly had to agree that they wouldn't be involved in the birth program. Just makes things less complicated."

"So, no drinking and no fucking for everyone else," Virge chuckled derisively, "Anyone with half a brain would've knocked that back." He glanced up at Elroy with a grin in between his grizzled beard, "Guess you had to raise your recruitment bar *real* low."

"That's probably the only part of all this that makes sense," Jesse joined in on belittling the bald raider, "I know I wouldn't want people like this guy fucking up the gene pool."

"Yeah, keep talking, assholes," Elroy grunted, his hand dropping to the revolver holstered on his waist.

"My father insisted that we only use donors from outside the community," Doctor Quinn idly cut across the tension building in the room. "In order to raise the next generation of people properly – who follow orders without question, who would sacrifice themselves for the greater good without hesitation – we can't allow anyone who would care about the progeny's welfare to interrupt their development."

"So you're gonna take every child away from their parents?" Riley asked, unable to imagine the heartache of a newborn baby being torn from its mother's arms.

Just when she had thought that the cult's misguided ideals couldn't have gotten any worse, she had to force herself to swallow another wave of nausea.

"Well, when ya put it like that," Shepherd began in his warm neighborly tone, "It tends to rub people the wrong way. Just think of it as building human robots. We take them off the production line, do a little programming, and away they go."

"Sounds familiar," Virge grunted, the grizzled war veteran scowling at the nurses.

"What's the point of all this?" Jesse asked curiously. Despite trying to hide his attempts at breaking out of his bonds behind his back, he couldn't help but wonder what their end goal was, "Do you think you're just gonna breed the country back to normal?"

"Raising a new generation was just phase one of my father's plan," Alyssa answered as she perked up again, her interest in the conversation renewed. "Just as he predicted the asteroid's impact, he also said that there would come a time when we would need soldiers who would be willing to put the survival of the human race above their own personal lives."

"No attachments, no emotions," Elroy added in reverent awe at the idea, "Just pure fucking machines ready for orders."

"We've selected our donors with strict screening criteria in place," Quinn continued, gesturing towards the six observation rooms on either side of the lab. "No physical or mental disabilities, no hereditary diseases, and most notably, heightened muscle retention – because the progeny are going to need every advantage they can get."

"Is the screening criteria the same for the women?" Riley wondered, remembering that Sterling's wife was dependent on medication for her thyroid condition.

If they had rejected Abbie Granger, then Sterling was in trouble – wherever he was.

"We make do with what we have," Alyssa adjusted her glasses as she looked over at Riley, studying the curves of her hips. "Beggars can't be choosers, but with one half of the equation perfect, theoretically, we can rely on having at least half the success rate."

"So you're building an army of super soldiers," Virge concluded, eyeing Doctor Quinn with his scrutinizing squint.

"What the fuck for?"

The nurses around the room shifted uneasily, and Shepherd whistled as he shot a sidelong glance at Alyssa.

"That's the one thing my father didn't mention," Quinn clasped her hands together in her lap as she looked at each of them in turn. "We don't know yet."

CHAPTER 35

"TALK ABOUT A FUCKING CULT!!" Riley Armstrong shouted, her outrage reverberating around the room. "You've been massacring and kidnapping people for your sick fucking breeding program, and you don't even know what the hell it's all for!?"

"In order to ensure the longevity of the human race," Alyssa Quinn calmly replied, quoting her father with a nostalgic smile, "We must be willing to set aside our own humanity."

"Trust the process," Shepherd nodded, silently gesturing for the apprehensive nurses to resume monitoring the hospital ward's medical equipment.

As much as Riley missed her own father, she couldn't imagine the thought of blindly committing such deplorable atrocities against other human beings for the sake of keeping his legacy alive.

Whatever childhood trauma that had impacted Alyssa back when she was young and impressionable, it had clearly cut her deep – down to the bone – and surrounding herself with psychopathic sycophants like Braxton Shepherd had allowed her wound to fester.

"Imagine if all this has been for nothing," Jesse chuckled, happily ridiculing Doctor Quinn's life's work. "When the government finally gets their shit together, they're gonna find out about this place, and then the whole country's gonna come down on your heads like a ton of bricks."

"Don't be so sure, kid," Virge grumbled, brooding in his chair. "Breeding super soldiers in a secret setup like this – top brass would be lining up like it's happy hour at the whorehouse just to take notes."

A chorus of heavy boots squeaked over the vinyl floor as Sterling appeared at the ward's entrance, escorted by the same four guards he had left with.

Ashen-faced, he found the nearest office chair and sank down into the seat, unable to look at any of them in the eye.

"Did you find your wife?" Riley asked, venturing closer to see that his hands had been cut loose.

"My wife?" Sterling echoed distractedly, as if he had only heard half of the question. "She's – yeah, my Abbie, she's fine." He lifted his head slightly, glancing up at the pair of medicine cabinets lining the back wall of the lab. "She's well taken care of. Got all the meds she needs."

"That's good to hear she's doing okay," Riley glanced hesitantly at Jesse and Virge, who both looked as equally as reluctant to raise the question that she was about to ask. "Sterling, did she tell you what's happening here?"

Granger swallowed.

He took a deep breath.

Rubbing at the dark circles underneath his eyes, he finally met her gaze.

"Yeah, she did," he answered, sitting up in his chair. "And I gotta say, this place is probably the best thing we could've asked for, ever since the shit hit the fan."

Shepherd caught the four guards' attention with a wave, and silently gestured for them to leave.

Elroy perked up with a finger on his chest, but deflated immediately at a small shake of the head from Braxton.

"So let me get this straight, you fucking pussy," Virge's dog tags jingled as he rounded on his friend. "You came to me blubbering, half dead, with your brother's blood on your hands, after you buried him and who knows how many others... *begging* me for my help. I didn't have to do shit. I didn't know you. I didn't have to get caught up in all this. I could've picked you off from a distance and saved myself the headache."

"I'm glad you didn't," Granger mumbled, his dark eyes dropping to the floor.

"I'm not," he wheeled his chair beside Sterling, scowling into the man's face. "This whole time, I thought – fuck it, may as well do some good before my number's up. Help a man save his wife from being passed around by a bunch of animals – and maybe save a shitload more while I'm at it? Yeah, that'd do it. That's my ticket through the pearly gates. But now we find out that the women are the ones doing the raping, all of a sudden, it's fine? Fuck you. You're a fucking coward."

Virge spat at his boots in contempt before wheeling away.

"How the hell are you comfortable with this?" Riley furrowed her eyebrows in disgust. "Your wife's gonna be carrying another man's child. Does your marriage mean nothing? Is she really not that important to you?"

"She is *everything* to me," fury flashed in Sterling's eyes as he rose to her challenge. He took a moment to breathe before addressing her again, "Fuck no, I'm not comfortable with this. But I'd do anything for my Abbie. We might not be able to get the meds she needs anywhere else. I mean, where else are we gonna go? Scavenging from place to place, struggling to survive, and hoping to find a drug store that hasn't already been looted? And even if we do, then eventually, if we stay out there long enough, we're gonna run into some bad people who are a whole lot worse than Shepherd and Quinn."

Alyssa relished in his admission as the room fell silent.

The nurses' shoes scuffed the vinyl floor as they paced back and forth, leaning over medical devices, flipping charts and comparing notes. And underneath the babble of bleeps, a faint scratching sound emanated from the desk that Jesse was leaning back against.

Doctor Quinn rose to her feet and bent over the intercom's workstation, thumbing the microphone's button.

"Numbers forty-seven and forty-eight," her voice called over the intercom, "Report to the lab, please. Numbers forty-seven and forty-eight."

Riley's heart sank.

She knew that forty-seven was Aunt Lorraine's number, and if she was sharing a room with her sister, then forty-eight could be none other than Susan Armstrong.

If Riley saw the pair of them now, she wouldn't know what to say.

"Our offer still stands," Shepherd spread his hands with a friendly smile. "If you're willing to earn your keep, there's a place here for each of ya." He nodded at Jesse, "I don't think I caught your name, son, but I'm willing to bet you'd do just fine out on that lake with a fishing rod. Sterling, ya look like a man who would do well on one of our response teams – maybe even lead one yourself someday. And Virge, I'd venture to guess ya know your way around a radio. We've got a comms room here if –"

"I got a better idea," the grizzled war veteran grunted. "Put me in charge of the armory."

"I'm gonna have to say no on that one," Braxton chuckled at the old man's sense of humor.

"Comms room's a fucking breeze," Elroy said to nobody in particular. "Shit, I'll take it if he doesn't want it."

"Who asked you, Beard Rash?" Virge narrowed his eyes at the bald raider. He turned back towards Shepherd, "You're asking me to help you find new people for you to kill and kidnap? Go fuck yourself. I'd rather watch your nice big house burn to the ground."

"Then you'll never get the opportunity," Alyssa clasped her hands together, standing behind the microphone with her eyebrows raised. "There's no place available here for anyone who isn't willing to contribute."

"What about me?" Riley asked, looking from Shepherd to Quinn. "If I stayed, what would my job be?"

"I thought that would be quite obvious," Quinn answered, stifling another smirk as she met Riley's gaze. "You're of child birthing age."

"Not a fucking chance," she stared daggers at the doctor. "So what happens now?"

"You have every right to refuse," Alyssa shrugged indifferently, "As did the rest of the women who came from your group. However, if you must insist on following your friend, Virge, out on the road to ruin, I'll still allow you to choose one person to leave with you – as long as that person chooses to leave. And in exchange, I expect the both of you to call off any other attacks that the rest of your group has been planning."

"What other attacks?" Sterling raised his head in confusion.

"What group?"

Riley's face dropped.

She had just lost her leverage.

CHAPTER 36

"Clever," Alyssa Quinn admitted, nodding in deference. "Had I been in your position, I might have said the same thing."

"You're too much of a crazy bitch to be in my position," Riley Armstrong shot back, glowering at the doctor. "I'm still taking my mom with me."

"You can try," Quinn snorted shamelessly, clasping her hands together with a haughty smirk. "But your chances of convincing her were never that high to begin with. What makes you even think that she'll want to leave with you?"

Because I'm her daughter, Riley wanted to say, but it was such a pitiful argument that she didn't even bother opening her mouth.

Instead, she seethed in silence.

The faint scratching sound of Jesse cutting away at his bonds had stopped.

Sterling was idly rotating his wedding ring around his finger.

Even Virge was feeling sorry for himself in the wake of his outburst.

Riley exhaled in exasperation, frustrated at how easily they were leaning towards accepting Shepherd's offer.

Grandma Eleanor, Keith Bowman, Hayden Marsh and Greg Preston had already given their lives – along with Herb, the Bradford Brothers, and all the other people who had died in Clementine – believing that Shepherd's men were just mindless monsters without a purpose.

Had they all known what kind of place this really was, prior to inviting Braxton and his brainwashed followers to their settlements, maybe things would have been different.

Or maybe they would have played out exactly the same way.

Regardless of what could have happened, there was at least one death that would have been preventable – Hayden's.

Riley looked over at the pair of medicine cabinets along the back wall of the lab, swallowing her sorrow. Even if his wound from the mountain lion's attack had been infected, they could have easily brought him here for proper medical treatment and prevented his needless death.

She considered that maybe it was time to stop fighting.

All she had managed to do was get other people killed.

Her body was almost broken, her fingers were lacerated and her pelvis was aching.

There was nothing left to give, and yet she knew, deep down to her very core, that if she accepted their offer to stay here, taking incapacitated men against their will, until she fell pregnant with a child that she could never keep, she would crush her own spirit and sink into a black void that she would never be able to crawl back out of again.

A pair of footsteps sounded from the corridor, shoes squeaking over the vinyl floor.

Riley turned to see her mother and aunt entering the lab together, both of them walking free and eager.

Lorraine was dressed in a bathrobe and slippers, still wearing her blissful smile from before. Her hair was wet from the shower after her romp in Room D, but she was still as greasy as ever.

"Riley!?" Susan Armstrong exclaimed, rushing across the room towards her daughter to sweep her up into a tight embrace. She smelled fresh and clean as she kissed Riley's grimy cheek before fussing over her, "Are you okay? After that fire broke out into the forest, I was worried we'd never see you again!"

With her bandaged hands still bound behind her back, Riley wanted nothing more than to soften in her mother's arms, surrendering to her nurturing tenderness.

But she knew that if she showed any sign of vulnerability – any weakness – she would never be able to lead her mother out of this madness.

Riley abruptly shrugged out of the embrace, struggling to maintain her composure against the confusion and hurt on her mother's face.

Swallowing the lump building in her throat, Riley backpedaled until she collided with the door to Room D.

Clumsily catching hold of the handle with her bound and bandaged hands, she pushed the door open and sidled inside.

"Please, no more!" the handcuffed man shrieked the instant he caught sight of her entering the room. Struggling against his restraints, he pleaded with the male nurse attending to him, "It's too soon! I'm not ready – I've never been ready! Please, I don't want it. No more, please. Just kill me. Just kill me… JUST FUCKING KILL ME!!"

"What do you think you're doing?" Doctor Quinn approached the observation room with Elroy in tow.

Riley played the last card she had left.

"If you want me to stay in this place," she began, narrowing her eyes at the doctor, "Then you'll have to convince me in here, in front of one of your victims."

"One of our *donors*," Alyssa corrected her, overlooking the lack of choice that they had given the patient. "Very well, I'll allow it – if only to help you sleep at night after you make the obvious decision. But if you make one wrong move while we're in there, I'll have Elroy kill your friends and blow your kneecaps. I don't imagine you'll have any trouble making your decision then."

"It doesn't need to come to that," Susan reassured the doctor before going to her daughter in the observation room. "I can convince her. Just give me some time to talk to her."

"I'm her aunt, I should be in there with them," Lorraine swelled with her own sense of self importance as she sauntered in after her sister. She shot a wink at the shirtless black man on the hospital bed, to his shuddering revulsion.

"If our lives are on the line," Sterling looked up from his seat, glancing over at Jesse and Virge before turning back to Quinn, "You need to give us a fighting chance. I didn't come all this way to get killed just because a teenage girl decided to lash out. If she tries anything, I'd prefer to be in there to stop her."

"At least one of you is on board with the program," Quinn replied, giving him her nod of approval before turning to Shepherd, "Braxton, I want you by the intercom, just in case."

"I don't think these guys are gonna give us any trouble," Shepherd folded his arms over his belly with a friendly smile. "While you're in there, I'm gonna see if I can't convince old Virge to change his mind."

The grizzled war veteran muttered a string of curses under his breath as Sterling, Alyssa and Elroy filed into Room D, joining Riley, Susan and Lorraine as they watched the male nurse tending to the patient.

"Riley…" Susan began as the door closed.

"Save it," she silenced her mother with a cold stare.

Riley had to remind herself that for the women who had chosen to join the cult community, they weren't just mothers, sisters and wives anymore. They were spineless fiends who had agreed to rape imprisoned men in exchange for their own comfort and convenience.

Before any of them could speak, Riley turned to the man in handcuffs.

"Where are you from?" she asked him in a gentle voice.

"What does it matter?" he moaned, mournfully rattling his restraints against the bed frame.

"Because I want them to remember that you're still a person," Riley replied, narrowing her eyes at Doctor Quinn.

"We c-came from Redhurst… California," he stammered, glancing around at everyone in the room with wide fearful eyes.

"Redhurst," she repeated, shaking her head at Susan. For all they knew, he could have been living in the same neighborhood. "How did you get here?"

"I never even wanted to leave our house," the man shut his red-rimmed eyes as a fresh tear traced the wet track down his cheek. "The asteroid didn't land anywhere near us, but the riots… Every day, we heard windows breaking, screams and gunshots. It only got worse at night. It wasn't safe to go out, but in the early days, our basement was fully stocked. Eventually we ran outta food though, and we didn't have a choice. Loni's parents live on the East Coast. We had enough fuel stashed to make it, and we thought we'd be safe as long as we stayed off the main roads, but we were *so hungry*. We thought we were gonna die of starvation on the highway until we heard that man's message on the radio."

"Shepherd," Riley knew, his name leaving a bitter taste in her mouth.

"We were so happy when we met him," the prisoner's voice cracked as he continued, his bottom lip quivering into a pained smile at the recollection. "For the first time in months, there was a normal human being, offering food, water and shelter to strangers in need. They brought us back here, fed us, interviewed us, took some blood samples... Loni thought it was weird, but I said everything's gonna be fine. Everything's gonna be okay."

He broke into a fresh sob, his handcuffs jolting against the bed frame.

"And then they shot him," tears streamed down his face as he opened his eyes again, blearily glaring at Quinn standing across the room in her white lab coat. He moaned in torment, spiraling back into his waking nightmare, "They shot my husband and pumped me full of some drug cocktail. Now I got bitches raping me every time their fucking drugs kick in!" His red-rimmed eyes looked up at his IV bag with loathing. He turned to Riley, and his anger turned into anguish, "I'm nothing but a piece of meat to them. I don't even wanna escape this hellhole anymore. I just want it to be over. Please, just kill me... FUCKING KILL ME!!"

Doctor Quinn motioned for the nurse to administer a sedative into the man's IV bag.

Riley stared around at them all as his feeble whimpers died down into silence.

Susan couldn't look her in the eye.

223

Lorraine shifted her weight uneasily.

"All this time, we thought our families were the victims," Riley turned her hard gaze on Sterling. "But look at this man. Look at what they've done to him. Your wife. My own mother. They've brutalized him. Don't tell me you're in support of this. They're *using* him, Sterling – exactly the same way we thought *they* were being used."

"Riley, it's the only way they'll let us stay here," Susan took her by the arms, trying to make her daughter see things from their perspective. "This is the best thing we could've hoped for. We don't have a choice."

"That's bullshit!" Riley shouted, jerking out of her mother's grip. "Quinn said you had every right to refuse. You could've walked away from all this. I can't believe you. They threw you into the back of that truck *yesterday fucking morning*, and now you're raping broken men just so that you can give birth to a bastard child and hand it over to a cult!? I feel sick just knowing we're related to each other."

Susan drew in a sharp breath, as if she had been stabbed through the heart.

Her eyes fell to the floor, and she turned to face the corner of the room, leaning against the wall for support.

"Now you've done it," Lorraine shook her head at Riley, disdainfully clucking her tongue before moving to console her shaking sister.

"I admire your sense of morality, Riley," Alyssa spoke over Susan's soft sobs. "And I agree with you – to an extent. What we're doing here isn't right. But it's necessary. You'll see. Years from now, the good that we'll have achieved here will outweigh the bad that we've done, and you'll be proud to have been a part of this. Or you might not. You might regret it. But at least

224

you'll be *alive*, along with the rest of the entire human race."

"You still don't get it," Riley would have pitied the delusional woman, if only the crazy bitch hadn't been the cause of so much suffering. "You've taken advantage of desperate people in need and torn their families apart. You've started a cult, and you've incited people to murder, kidnap and rape, all because your dad guessed – fucking *guessed* – that one day, an asteroid would hit the planet. You talk about raising a new generation of super soldiers, and for what? You don't even fucking know!!"

She took a menacing step towards Quinn, and Elroy's hand dropped to the revolver holstered on his waist.

"Wait, hold on!" Sterling held up his hands, placing himself between them, "Just – hear me out. Riley, all you want is for the abuse to stop, right?"

"And I want my mom back," she answered bitterly, despite what her mother had done. Her eyes narrowed at the bald raider's revolver next, "And I want Elroy's head too, for killing my grandma."

"One thing at a time," Sterling glanced back at Elroy, silently pleading for the man to keep his weapon holstered. "Quinn, this is your house, your rules. You said you need pregnant women, cool. Whatever it's all for, I don't care. My wife needs her meds, so this is where we're gonna stay. We'll do whatever you want us to do."

"Thank you," the refined blonde doctor nodded at his submission, "I appreciate your –"

"But you also said," Sterling held up a respectful hand as he continued, "That these men aren't victims. They're donors, right? Well, if all you need is their *donations*, why not store their sperm – I'm sure you've got the equipment for it – and then impregnate the women using IVF instead?"

Alyssa clasped her hands together as she cocked her head to the side in consideration.

"Fucking test tube babies!?" Lorraine burst out, whirling around to glower at Sterling for daring to even make the suggestion. "Way to make us women feel like a bunch of lab rats!" She turned to Quinn, "Don't tell me you're actually taking him seriously. I know I've only been here for one day, but I've made a lot of friends, and *everyone* prefers the old-fashioned way. I'll bet even some of the donors are loving their new lives. So will this guy, eventually," she waved her hand at the sedated man cuffed to the hospital bed. "He's just sad because his husband died, that's all. He'll get over it. I mean, it's not like he's gonna be cheating on him."

"You have no shame," Riley furrowed her eyebrows at her aunt in disgust. "Everything you just said was wrong on so many levels, but you wanna know the biggest thing that stood out? The idea that a person as selfish as you could ever make any friends."

"I can't deal with this," Lorraine threw up her hands in exasperation. "You're stressing me out. I feel like I'm gonna have a panic attack."

She fanned her face as she began to hyperventilate.

"Take it easy, just breathe," the male nurse came to Lorraine's side in a flash, glancing sidelong at Doctor Quinn. "Maybe she's right. Maybe we should leave things exactly the way they are. If they're gonna get stressed out like this, they'll be less likely to conceive."

"You're a lying piece of shit, Lorraine," Riley spat, momentarily feeling her father's presence in the room, as if Nolan Armstrong's spirit was finally confronting his contemptible sister-in-law through his daughter. "You're a grown-ass woman and you're acting like a child. Have some fucking dignity."

"I understand why you're upset, Riley," Susan broke in, brushing her tear-stained cheeks. "And you're right. What these people are doing here is wrong. But I'm convinced that – regardless of whatever happens in the future – right now, this is the best place for us to survive the apocalypse."

"My Abbie said the same thing to me," Sterling nodded solemnly, as heavy as the truth was weighing down on his shoulders. "As long as we stay here, doing whatever they ask us to do, we'll be taken care of. We won't want for anything."

Riley wasn't convinced.

This wasn't surviving.

This was dying, each of them suffering slow and terrible deaths while their bodies lived on to bear witness.

She glared at Granger – once the lone gunman garbed in green – now bereft of his guns and what was left of her respect.

"Shut up, you fucking cuck," Riley jeered at him before turning to her mother. "What would Dad say if he saw the monster you've become?"

Without warning, Susan slapped her hard across the face.

"Riley! I'm so sorry," she instantly clapped her hands to her mouth, staring horror-struck at the angry red mark on her daughter's cheek. "Your father, he'd – he would want us both to be safe and provided for."

With her bandaged hands bound behind her back, Riley couldn't even rub at the stinging pain on her cheek.

"Not like this," she scowled back at her mother. "I don't want any part of this."

"Sounds like you've made your decision, then," Doctor

Quinn concluded in disappointment. "Now live with it."

CHAPTER 37

Riley Armstrong stepped back into the lab, with Elroy watching warily as the bald raider stood to one side, his hand resting on the revolver holstered on his waist.

"Please, think about what you're doing!" Susan called after her daughter, begging for her to reconsider. She turned to Alyssa, "Doctor Quinn, if you could just give me some more time, I'm sure she'll come around."

"I know one thing that might change her mind," Lorraine murmured suggestively. "Why don't we let that Hayden boy knock her up? If he's still around, he'd make an excellent donor. This one time, I *accidentally* walked in on him while he was in the shower, and…"

Riley suppressed the urge to gag as she noticed Virge Norton sitting beside Room D's doorway, having wheeled himself over to listen in on their conversation.

"Stiff shit, kid," the grizzled war veteran grumbled as he scowled across the room, "Didn't go much better out here either."

She followed his gaze past the cluster of nurses and medical equipment.

Jesse Bowman was still leaning back against one of the desks as he chatted idly with Shepherd.

"All I'm saying is," Jesse croaked, licking his cracked lips, "If I could knock back a couple drinks while I'm out fishing, then the whole idea of staying here would sound a hell of a lot better."

"I know what ya mean, son," Braxton chuckled in his office chair, "But if we let the fishermen drink, pretty soon, everybody's gonna be out on that lake – me included – and nothing would ever get done. But listen, if there's anything else I can do to sweeten the deal, I'm all ears!"

"Well, there is one other thing…" Jesse supposed, glancing over at Riley before turning away. "That jacket you're wearing – I don't really have any clothes on me besides this shitty red shirt."

"Well, I dunno if this is gonna fit ya," Shepherd looked down at Nolan Armstrong's fur-lined leather aviator jacket, the civil snake having stolen it from Keith Bowman's corpse. "But if that's what it's gonna take to convince ya, then why not? You're gonna need it anyway – it sure gets cold out on that lake in the winter."

Riley's shoulders slumped in defeat.

Jesse was joining the cult for a jacket.

Susan, Lorraine and Sterling weren't going anywhere.

It was just her and Virge left now.

She took a deep breath, coming to grips with their new reality.

"Come on, we're leaving," Riley sighed, turning to Virge.

"Damn straight we are," he replied, his wary gaze sliding sideways as the others began filing out of the observation room.

He waited until he caught sight of Doctor Quinn's white lab coat, and with a flurry of movement, he spun his wheelchair and hooked a hard fist into the blonde woman's navel, driving out all of the refinement and poise from the doctor's doubled-over body.

"Get Beard Rash, quick!" Virge grunted as he wrestled the reeling Quinn onto the vinyl floor, his fingers scrabbling for the set of keys in her back pocket.

Icy adrenaline shot through Riley's veins, and she lurched over the fallen woman, headbutting Elroy in the center of his rash-ridden chin before he had a chance to draw his weapon.

Stunned and disoriented, the bald raider staggered backwards into the observation room, his arms pinwheeling as he fell to the floor.

Riley stood frozen in the doorway, her hands still bound behind her back.

Her mind was drawing a blank for her next move as Elroy groggily reached for his revolver.

Suddenly, she was shoved aside, and her mother bolted into the room.

"You killed Ma!" Susan shouted with tears of rage in her eyes, leaping on top of Elroy to grapple with his arm. "I won't let you take my baby girl!!"

Lorraine shrieked in the chaos as the nurses huddled together, not knowing what else to do. Even Sterling had his back against the wall, hesitant to choose a side.

"My dad was wearing that yesterday," Jesse declared across the room, glancing pointedly at the jacket that Shepherd had placed on the desk, "Until your men killed him."

Jesse drew his arms out from behind his back, revealing that he had severed his bonds with a pair of scissors clutched in his hand.

"Hold on, now," Braxton's voice was taut with tension as he backed away, holding his hands up in surrender. "Take it easy, son."

"STOP CALLING ME SON!!" Jesse snapped, chasing Shepherd to the intercom's workstation and latching onto him from behind.

Before Braxton could reach the microphone, Jesse plunged the pair of scissors into the side of his neck.

"You lying piece of shit!" Jesse yelled over the nurses' panicked screams, stabbing and slashing the gurgling glib-tongued son of a bitch in a frenzy of cathartic release. "Fuck you, Shepherd! Fuck you, Stuart! This is for my dad!!"

A sharp metal *thwack* resounded from inside Room D, the male nurse holding the shirtless prisoner's IV pole as he stood over Susan Armstrong's limp body.

Elroy shoved the dazed woman to the side, just in time to see Riley hurling herself like a ragdoll at the bald raider on the floor, burying her elbow into his sternum.

Hacking and wheezing in the tangled mess of bodies, Elroy finally managed to unholster his revolver.

"All I wanted was the fucking day off!" he yelled as he drew up on his knees, holding his weapon by the barrel over her head.

Riley saw the pistol whip coming, and on instinct, she moved her arms to block the blow.

The flash of metal came down in slow motion as she remembered – too late – that her hands were still tied behind her back.

CHAPTER 38

Black stars of pain swam in the corners of Riley Armstrong's eyes, her jaw slack with the coppery taste of defeat in her mouth.

Susan was lying on her side, blinking groggily at the observation room's hospital bed, as if she was seeing it for the first time.

The male nurse was hunched over the handcuffed prisoner, busily trying to reattach the IV pole's connections that had come loose.

Wheezing from the blow to his sternum, Elroy clambered to his feet and lumbered over to the doorway with his revolver in hand.

Remembering Jesse and Virge, Riley struggled to sit upright, but with her hands bound behind her back, the searing pain in her strained groin made it impossible to get back onto her feet using her legs alone.

Still determined to make a difference, she rolled over onto her back instead, desperately worming her way across the vinyl floor towards the exit.

Lorraine was screaming in horror, her eyes filled with the

sight of Braxton Shepherd's blood spreading across the floor.

Half of the nurses fled the lab in their panic, but one man was sneaking up behind Jesse with a syringe.

Finally making up his mind, Sterling joined the fight.

With a guttural roar, he tackled the nurse backwards into a desk before brutally beating him over the head with his fist and a keyboard, sending buttons and teeth scattering across the room.

"Elroy!" Doctor Quinn panted, still reeling on her hands and knees. "Do your fucking job!!"

The bald raider staggered out from the observation room's doorway, but before he could level his revolver at Sterling, a bodybuilder surged out from Room E with a murderous gleam in his eyes. The muscle-bound man flipped tables, charts and medical equipment as he barreled towards the two remaining nurses in the lab.

Virge zoomed out of Room E on the big man's heels, taking a hard turn as his arms raced towards Room F with Alyssa's keys in his lap.

Lorraine cowered behind a desk as Elroy rapidly switched between targets.

He took a rushed shot at Jesse and Sterling, both of them ducking to the floor as the bullet punched a hole through a computer screen.

At the sound of a shriek from across the room, the bald raider turned his attention back to the bodybuilder as he threw one of the nurses through Room B's window.

The next bullet hit the muscle-bound man in his back, but it wasn't enough to stop him from grabbing the second nurse in a bear hug from behind, carrying her kicking and screaming.

"SAY HI TO MY COUSINS, BITCH!!" he roared, before

raking the woman's throat across the broken window's jagged glass.

Elroy was lining up another shot, when Sterling seized his opportunity, charging out from behind the desks and knocking the revolver from the bald raider's hand, the two men trading savage blows.

Riley and Alyssa locked eyes for a split second before they scrambled for the fallen gun, Quinn crawling on her hands and knees while Riley pushed herself along the vinyl floor with her squirming feet.

Racing neck and neck, but with no hope of reaching the gun before Quinn, Riley forced herself to do the unthinkable.

In a fit of desperation, she lunged for the doctor's arm, taking a bite out of her wrist.

She clamped her jaws tight, *squeezing*, until she felt a warm gush of blood flooding into her mouth.

Alyssa screeched in agony as she collapsed onto her elbows, clutching her arm above the wound to staunch the flow of blood.

Riley spat the crimson paste into the woman's twisted face for good measure, blinding Quinn before resuming her writhing wriggle across the floor towards the gun.

Elroy's face was a bloody mess, but he had Sterling pinned down on one of the desks, raining hammer fists down onto his chest.

Jesse rushed towards the bald raider with his pair of scissors raised, when the male nurse from Room D burst through the open doorway, knocking him to the floor.

Riley's bandaged fingers fumbled with the revolver behind her back, doing her best to find the firearm's handle without shooting herself.

She wrapped one of her clumsy hands around the hilt and lifted her hips up off the floor, taking a blind guess at where she was aiming the pistol.

CRACK!

Elroy bellowed in pain as a shot from his own revolver shredded through his kneecap. His legs buckled and he collapsed onto the floor, only to receive another searing hot slug down the side of his face, burying into his collarbone.

Riley adjusted her aim just slightly, staring at the bald raider dead in the eye – filling her heart with hate for the man who had executed her grandmother – and smiling as she fired one last time, emptying the revolver into his face.

"Take the rest of the day off, bitch," she exhaled before glancing over at Quinn, who was still preoccupied with treating her wrist wound.

Jesse rose from behind a workstation, breathing hard, his forearms spattered with blood. He stepped over the bodies of the slain medical staff as he made his way towards Riley.

"Want me to cut you free?" he panted, brandishing the bloody pair of scissors as he dropped to his knees beside her.

"No, I thought I'd hang out like this for the rest of the day," she gave him a stupid answer to his stupid question before dropping the gun and rolling over onto her stomach.

He snorted as he began sawing through her bonds, the scissors slippery with blood.

Alyssa finished tying off her wounded wrist with her white lab coat before fixing her glasses. Wiping the blood from her lenses, her pupils dilated at the sight of Shepherd and Elroy dead, along with all of the nurses who had stayed behind.

Realizing that she had lost control of the lab, she crawled away towards the nearest workstation, her shoes disappearing behind a row of desks.

Listless after the beating from Elroy, Sterling slumped off the table, one hand holding his battered chest as he stumbled towards the pair of medicine cabinets along the back wall.

Virge pushed himself across the lab towards the other three observation rooms, dodging the bodybuilder as the muscle-bound man began destroying the medical equipment, sparks flying from smashed screens and ripped cables.

"STOP IT!!" Lorraine screamed as she emerged from her hiding place. She glowered at Riley, "You're ruining everything! Why couldn't you and your friends just leave us alone!? We were happy here. For once in my life, I was actually happy!!"

Nobody paid her any attention.

Sterling raided the medical cabinets, scanning the names of pill bottles before sweeping entire shelves into a satchel.

"Can anyone hear me?" Lorraine asked, her tone taking on a tinnier quality.

"We can hear you," Riley huffed at the vinyl floor as Jesse continued cutting away at her bonds. "We just don't – LORRAINE, WHAT THE FUCK ARE YOU DOING!?"

"They're trying to escape," Lorraine had her thumb on the microphone's button, her voice carrying over the intercom. "Everyone report to the lab, please."

CHAPTER 39

"You stupid fucking idiot!!" Riley Armstrong shouted, looking up at her aunt with loathing.

"Can somebody shoot that dumb bitch!?" Virge yelled as he zoomed in and out of the lab into the next observation room, still releasing the prisoners.

Lorraine Tipton shrank away from the microphone, silently trembling after the announcement that had doomed them all to die, or worse.

"What the hell are we gonna do?" Riley wondered aloud, still lying flat on her stomach.

She glanced at the revolver by her side before turning her head towards the corridor, dreading the thought of the rest of the guards storming into the lab at any moment.

Even if Elroy had been carrying any spare bullets on him, six rounds at a time wasn't going to cut it.

"I'm almost through," Jesse grunted through gritted teeth, still sawing at her bonds with the bloody pair of scissors. "There's another door along the back wall – I say we see where it takes us."

"I've gotta get my wife first," Sterling called over his shoulder as he emptied out the second medicine cabinet.

The bare feet of a man wearing scrub pants padded across the vinyl floor, stopping beside Riley. Lying on her stomach, she couldn't see his face, but she could see that he was shirtless.

The beefy freed prisoner picked up the revolver.

Who's this fucking hero? Riley thought to herself.

The cords binding her wrists finally snapped free, and she gave a sigh of relief as her shoulders rolled forward.

"Done," Jesse declared proudly, before gasping, "What the – I thought you were dead…?"

Riley's heart skipped a beat, and her eyebrows furrowed at the floor as she wondered who it could be.

She pushed herself back onto her knees, grimacing at the pain in her lacerated fingers and her throbbing thighs.

Gazing up at the broad-shouldered man, her pupils dilated in disbelief.

"You don't look too happy to see me," his whiskey-cured voice filled the lab.

"No – no, no, no," Lorraine cowered before the revolver pointed squarely at her face. "Don't do this. Please, don't do this. I might be pregnant. *PLEASE!!*"

"If you are, I'm doing the kid a favor," the ghost of Keith Bowman squared his stubbled jaw, glowering at the deplorable woman with his stony gaze.

CRACK!

No regret.

No remorse.

He simply watched Lorraine's body as it flopped onto the floor.

"Lorraine!?" Susan screamed in horror, stumbling out of Room D to see the hole blown through her sister's forehead.

Her eyes filled with tears as she mumbled, "Not you too. Not you too…"

Keith swept the gun's barrel towards Susan next.

"What the fuck are you doing!?" Riley lurched to her feet to knock his arm off target.

She wasn't fast enough, but it didn't matter.

The revolver gave up an impotent *click*.

"That's my mom, you fucking asshole!" Riley's relief to see that he was still alive had died the instant he had pulled the trigger.

"She might look like her," Keith's voice dripped with contempt, glowering at Susan. "But she's not the same woman I knew."

"Dad?" Jesse croaked as he rose to his feet, stretching his blood-spattered arms towards his father. "Riley said they killed you yesterday."

"Gonna take more than a couple sucker punches to keep me down," Keith replied, the scorn falling away from his face as he smiled at Jesse.

He dropped the gun to hug his son for the first time in months.

Susan knelt beside Lorraine's corpse, shaking with grief as she cradled her sister's head and sobbed up at the ceiling.

"When I said shoot that dumb bitch, I didn't mean actually shoot her," Virge paused in the doorway of Room B, squinting across the room at the pair of women on the vinyl floor.

"Trust me, we're better off," Riley replied, looking around the lab. "Did anyone see where Quinn went?"

Sprays of sparks erupted from the broken medical equipment as the bodybuilder continued his rampage across the room, with two more of the freed prisoners joining in, letting

240

loose the rage that had been bottled up inside them for who knew how long, ensuring that nobody else would ever suffer the horrific torment that they had endured.

A vibrating *thrum* reverberated around the lab as an electrical fire broke out, scattered charts igniting as the flames spread rapidly throughout the room.

"Fuck her, we're outta time," Jesse stepped away from Keith, grabbing the fur-lined leather aviator jacket and tossing it back to his father. "We've gotta go."

"Not without Abbie!" Sterling shouted, throwing the satchel of medicine over his shoulder. He ran past an exploding wall outlet, shielding his face through the billowing black smoke as he rushed towards the exit. "Get us a vehicle, we'll catch up!"

"I'm not letting these boys burn alive," Virge declared, resolutely rolling himself into the next observation room with the set of keys jingling in his lap.

"Mom, we need to go," Riley jerked back into motion, limping to her mother's side and tugging on her arm with her bandaged hands.

Overcome with bereavement, Susan was deaf to anything but the sound of her own mournful wails, and Riley was too weak to pull her mother to her feet.

"Shepherd! Doc Quinn!?" shouts came from the other side of the building as a group of guards entered the lodge.

"Jesse, Riley, there's a garage through there," Keith jerked his head towards the door along the back wall beside the medicine cabinets. He barked at the other freed prisoners, "Guys, if any of us are getting outta this place alive, we need to buy them some time!"

The former policeman zipped up the fur-lined leather aviator jacket, his beefy frame bulging underneath as he and the bodybuilder lifted a desk between them. Sharing a resolved nod, the two men charged through the black smoke clouding the corridor, with the other pair of escaping prisoners hard on their heels.

"Go, I've got her," Jesse assured Riley as he crouched beside Susan.

"Are you sure?" Riley furrowed her eyebrows as she studied his face, remembering that he still held Susan responsible for his mother's death.

"Riley, you can't lift her," he grunted as he tried to pry Susan's hands from her sister. "You can barely walk as it is. Now hurry up and grab us a car before we're all dead."

A burst of gunshots from the other side of the building added weight to his urgency.

She hated the idea of abandoning her mother in the middle of a fire, with only Jesse to get her out. But Hayden had believed that he might be good for something, and after everything that had happened over the past few days, it seemed that Jesse had finally proven himself worthy of a second chance.

Trusting him to lead Susan out alive, Riley staggered towards the back door, waving away puffs of black smoke as smashed screens sparked across the floor.

The whitewashed drywall surrounding the lab glowed red through the dark haze as the building's circuitry combusted.

She reached the back door and threw it wide, breathing in the stale air of the brick-lined garage as a cloud of smoke billowed out behind her.

There were five vehicles parked in the big garage, but Riley paused at the sound of a panicked murmur.

"Don't tell me I dropped it," the small voice rose from behind a charcoal gray suburban. "I had it in my pocket, and then... shit."

Riley rounded the rear of the suburban to see Doctor Quinn patting her pockets with her good hand.

She turned at the sound of Riley's sneakers, and for a fleeting moment, the two women locked eyes with each other, both of their hearts kicking into overdrive.

Alyssa bolted.

Lurching on aching legs, Riley chased her to the nearest roller door.

"Help!" Quinn screamed, mashing the door's button. "I'm in here!!"

Riley careened into the woman from behind, throwing both of their bodies against the corrugated steel of the rising roller door.

Quinn dropped to her hands and knees, gasping in pain as she remembered her wounded wrist. Down on her elbows instead, she tried to scramble underneath the opening garage door, but not before Riley slammed the door's button again and fell on top of her, pinning the doctor to the floor.

"You're not getting away with this, you crazy bitch!" Riley yelled as the roller door came down on the back of Quinn's neck.

The door's motor shuddered for a moment, before its safety measures engaged and the gears kicked into reverse, the corrugated steel bouncing back up.

"Somebody help me!" Quinn screamed again as she twisted around onto her back, her hands clawing at the garage door in an attempt to pull herself out from underneath Riley.

Snarling through the pain in her pelvis, Riley rose up on her knees and hooked her elbow around the door's crossbar, dropping her weight until the motor shuddered again.

"Don't do this!" Alyssa begged from outside as the corrugated steel jarred over her neck, the grimy weather seal flapping mere inches above her throat. Her thumb appeared under the roller door as she tried to hold it up with her good hand. "Please, you don't know what you're doing."

"I know exactly what I'm doing, and why I'm doing it," Riley snarled under the exertion of keeping Quinn pinned to the floor. She leaned back on the crossbar, trying to close the inches between the corrugated steel and the doctor's throat, when she caught sight of the garage door's emergency release handle dangling down. "That's a hell of a lot more than what I can say for you."

With every ounce of strength left in her body, Riley launched herself upwards and reached for the red cord.

Gripping and ripping, she disengaged the locks and brought the roller door down on Alyssa Quinn's throat.

"All I wanted to do… was help people," Alyssa gagged as her feet flailed across the floor.

"You still can," Riley breathed hard, wiping her mouth with the back of her hand as she collapsed beside the doctor's thrashing body. With one final burst of energy, she grabbed hold of Quinn's good hand and tore it from the garage door. "You can do everyone a favor, and fucking die!!"

Riley held the woman's arm to the floor, listening to her choke and sputter, watching her body spasm and kick, wondering how many innocent lives had been sacrificed in the name of her crazy cult's crackpot ideas.

She held down Alyssa's arm until her feet stopped twitching.

CHAPTER 40

"Oh, fuck," Jesse Bowman breathed as he and Susan Armstrong rounded the rear of the charcoal gray suburban.

"Riley!" Susan shrugged her arm from around Jesse's shoulders, coughing from the smoke as they both rushed to her side. "Are you okay?"

"I got her," Riley panted victoriously, nodding at Quinn's dead body as she tried to push herself back onto her feet.

Her knees jerked and dropped uselessly, utterly spent.

"Come on," Jesse grunted as he and Susan picked up Riley between the two of them.

"Jesse!" Keith's whiskey-cured voice reverberated around the brick-lined garage.

"Here, Dad," he called, holding the suburban's back door open so that they could lift Riley inside.

"Whole hellhole's about to go up in flames," Virge rolled into view with the front of his shirt drawn up over his nose. He spun his chair and tossed Keith the set of keys. "We need to get the fuck outta here."

"The guards have backed off," Keith jumped in behind the steering wheel, holding a pair of pistols in one hand and

Quinn's keys in the other. He glanced back at Riley before handing her a gun, "But we've still gotta get through them."

"You're better off giving me the gun," Virge said as he hoisted his legs up into the front passenger seat. "I know a thing or two about firing from a moving vehicle."

"I trust her with it more than I trust you," Keith replied, flipping through the keys. "Now sit back and shut up."

"I can feel the gratitude already," Virge grumbled before leaning out to grab his chair.

"We might not even need to shoot anyone," Susan spoke up as she slid across the backseat towards Riley. "The guards might think we're just the nurses trying to escape."

"With Quinn's head under the garage door?" Riley snorted as she rolled down her window and flipped the pistol's safety lever off. "I doubt the shit outta that."

"Everybody ready?" Keith barked as he switched on the ignition and punched the car into gear.

"Ready!" Jesse called back, flashing him a thumbs-up before stooping to lift the roller door.

"Wait!!" Sterling choked as he and his wife burst out of the black cloud of smoke billowing from the lab.

Keith popped the trunk and nodded at Jesse.

The roller door screeched open, flooding the garage with daylight as Jesse sprinted back towards the suburban. Meanwhile, Sterling and Abbie piled into the back, pulling the trunk shut behind them.

Keith gunned the engine and they roared out of the garage, the tires barely touching the surface of the driveway as they landed with a skidding crunch on the gravel cul-de-sac.

Then, as suddenly as they had taken off, Keith slammed the brakes, jerking everyone forward in their seats.

Riley leaned into her mother to see a wave of women streaming down the front stairs of the hulking wooden lodge, screaming and clutching their bellies as flames from the electrical fire swept across the entire house.

The other escaping prisoners were using the pack of pregnant women as human shields, only stopping to pick off one of the guards with a stolen gun before jumping back into the crowd.

Without any chain of command to keep them all in line, Shepherd's men gave into the chaos, the raiders breaking rank and chasing after the fleeing women.

Some of them were husbands reuniting with their wives – but only some.

The other guards either tackled the remaining women to the ground or hauled them back to the log cabins.

"Can't say I like it," Virge remarked as they listened to the screams, "But after seeing those boys chained up back there like that – well, karma's a real bitch."

"Doesn't make it right," Keith growled as he pointed his pistol out the window, taking aim at the pair of van-sized diesel generators rumbling away in the nearby clearing.

He squeezed off three shots before the generators fired back, going up in an explosion of twisted metal as the inferno's blast swallowed the air, sending the big neighboring wood shed's scorching timber flying into the rows of log cabins.

More shouts and screams of terror ensued as burning debris rained down over the cult community, crippling the morale of any other raider who was still concerned about keeping the place safe and restoring order.

Riley spotted Halsey among the crowd – unmistakable with his thick bandage wrapped across his broken nose.

He was unarmed, trying to shield one of the pregnant women from the soaring wreckage.

She held him in her gun's sights for a few dragging seconds, grappling with whether she should pull the trigger, until the shirtless bodybuilder surged out from the crowd and clotheslined him.

Halsey's feet lifted off the ground before he dropped like a plank of wood, and before she knew it, Riley was aiming her pistol at Chelsea Preston.

The blonde college girl breathed a sigh of relief as she stepped over the fallen raider, still wearing a bandage around her head as she waved back, flagging down the car.

"Riley, isn't that Chelsea?" Susan peered out the window as she eased her daughter's gun to the side. "Keith, we need to pick her up and find Katanya."

"We've got space here in the back," Sterling called from the trunk, he and his wife shifting to make room.

"No," Riley replied flatly, turning away as Chelsea faltered in the gravel cul-de-sac. "I agree with Virge. Karma's a real bitch. My grandma – and Greg, her own brother – died yesterday trying to protect her, and she's been living the good life here ever since? Fuck that. Same for Katanya. From now on, we take who we need, leave who we don't."

CHAPTER 41

Riley Armstrong rolled up her window against the fumes of Nebraska's burnt countryside.

They were cruising down the highway in the charcoal gray suburban, with Virge giving directions to Keith up front.

"Where'd you and Sterling come from anyway?" Keith asked, glancing sidelong at the grizzled war veteran.

"I'll tell you where I would've *liked* to come from," Virge scratched his beard with half a smile, "Chained up to a hospital bed in the middle of nowhere. Damn, if it was me in your place, I wouldn't have needed rescuing. And if you try telling me it was the worst weekend of your life, I'm calling you a fucking liar."

"Not all of them were bad," Keith conceded with a snort, "But you never met Lorraine."

Susan bristled in between Riley and Jesse, but she pursed her lips and let it go.

The Grangers spoke softly with each other in the back, glad to be together again as they rifled through Sterling's satchel, separating Abbie's thyroid medicine from the rest of the pill bottles.

"Well, whether you're happy about the rescue or not," Jesse tapped Keith on the shoulder from behind, "I'm glad you're still alive, Dad. And I'm sorry about being such a dick these past few months."

"Whatever happens, you're still my son," Keith accepted his apology, breathing a deep sigh of contentment before grinning up at the rearview mirror. "Just goes to show that being a dick runs in the family."

"Mom, are you okay?" Riley nudged her mother gently.

Susan glanced up at Keith's reflection before looking down at her lap again.

"I just need some time," she replied quietly, her face drawn.

Riley nodded her understanding.

She knew not to press her mother until she was ready to talk.

Everything had changed so much since they had left Redhurst.

Her father was gone.

Her grandmother was gone.

And now her aunt was gone too.

It was just Riley and her mother left in the family, and she wasn't even sure that she really knew who her mother was now.

But she could find out.

"Mom?" Riley prodded her again. "Could you tell me that story about how you and Dad met?"

* * *

Keep reading for an exclusive sneak peek at the next book -
Scavengers of The Fall.

Find out what happens next!

Thank you so much for reading Raiders of The Fall. I hope you enjoyed the story.

Join my newsletter here to receive an email when the next book gets published!
www.steveheuzinkveld.com/newsletter

I'd also like to invite you to my Book Lovers Facebook Group. Chat with me, have a character named after you, talk with other fans, and win exclusive prizes and giveaways.
Join the fun!
www.facebook.com/groups/SteveHeuzinkveldVIPFans

Here's a QR code so you don't have to type out any links:

Keep turning the pages for a sneak peek at the next book - Scavengers of The Fall.
Or continue reading on Amazon:

FIND OUT WHAT HAPPENS NEXT!

www.amazon.com/dp/B0BQZ9HF2G

ACKNOWLEDGMENTS

As always, first and foremost, I want to thank my beautiful wife, Hariezoy, for supporting me and encouraging me every single day, and for giving me the freedom to burn the midnight oil to hit the keyboard every night until the sun comes up.

A huge thanks also goes to my Patreon followers, Greg Hyndman, Rupert Lugo and Martin Georgiev. Your continued support has really helped soften the financial impact in hiring professional artists for my book covers, the ongoing website costs, and all of the other expenses that it takes to keep this author's dreams alive!

My heartfelt thanks to my Oma, Lena Heuzinkveld, who inspired my love for books at a young age. Sadly, she'll never be able to read this, but when I was writing the character of Eleanor Tipton, I felt so many similarities between her and Oma, along with her favorite phrase every time we complained about something trivial - "You never lived in a war." I hope there's a good bookstore up there in Heaven, although I'm not sure how I'll get this one on the shelves! Rest in peace, Oma.

I'd also like to thank my uncle, Dan Wynne, for his extensive knowledge on firearms, afforded to him from decades worth of experience in the industry.

And last but not least, thank you. As an independently-published author, this is very often a one-man show, and after the hours upon hours I've invested into this project, it means the world to me that you've taken the time to meet the characters living in my head.

I'd love to put your name here in my future books, right alongside Greg, Rupert and Martin. Join us on Patreon for access to never-before-seen chapters from my other works, as well as autographed copies of future books, all while helping me to bring more stories to life!

www.patreon.com/SteveHeuzinkveld

P.S. I love hearing from my fans - feel free to contact me any time!

-Steve
author@SteveHeuzinkveld.com
www.SteveHeuzinkveld.com

Preview - Scavengers of The Fall

"You're not gonna find something like this for a while," Keith Bowman grunted, dropping the dead woman's corpse onto the living room's carpet.

"Yeah, looks like you lucked out," Sterling Granger agreed, swinging another stiff up onto the couch. "Anything worth finding now is either buried or carried."

"I know, it just feels so tacky," Riley Armstrong replied as she drew weathered curtains across the room's broken window, giving them cover from the street.

She knew that the sight of the damp dirty canvas would only be announcing their presence in the bleak suburban neighborhood, but she figured that whoever had left the pair of bodies out on the road would have already noticed that something was amiss.

"Don't tell me you're getting squeamish over a dead give-away," Keith shot her a grin as he wrangled the backpack off the woman's corpse.

"*Dead giveaway*," Sterling echoed with a dry chuckle as he patted the pockets of the man with a hole in his chest. "Good one."

"Looting a corpse is one thing, but wearing its shoes…" Riley trailed off as she sank down to her knees anyway, pulling her gloves off before untying the dead woman's boots.

"Where do you think organ donations used to come from?" Keith asked rhetorically as he rummaged through the backpack, his grin souring as he fished out a smashed jar of preserves. He tossed the slimy shards aside before nodding at the pair of boots. "If it makes you feel any better, they can't smell any shittier than we do."

The first boot came off with a stubborn *thock*.

He was right.

If there was a stench coming from the cadaver's feet, it wasn't registering for Riley.

They had been living on the road for months, using whatever water they could find to drink rather than for showering.

The last time she had felt reasonably clean was a few weeks ago, after a quick plunge into a cold river. She had regretted it from the moment that she had resurfaced, the wintry wind reducing her to a bundle of shivering skin and bones until she got dressed again.

"Don't think about it – just put them on," Sterling looked up at her as he laid out his loot on the coffee table. "Your sneakers aren't gonna do you any good when winter really hits."

Riley bit her bottom lip as she examined the dead woman's shoes.

They were strong and sturdy, probably meant for hiking.

There was no doubt that they could survive slogging through the snowy weather.

And best of all, they were her size.

Holding the pair of boots upside down, she knocked them together a few times, half-expecting a clump of crawling maggots to fall out.

Nothing.

She breathed a small sigh of relief before summoning her resolve, kicking off her sneakers and slipping on the second-hand shoes.

"Congratulations," Keith gave her two mocking claps of applause. "I'd hate to see you shopping though. You only had one option and you still took your sweet ass time."

"Fuck you," Riley gave him a small snort, lacing up her new boots as she nodded at the backpack. "You find anything?"

"Half-empty packet of crackers," Keith stood up and kicked the bag over. "Can't eat it though. Not unless you want a blood-coated cracker sandwich." He looked over at Sterling. "What about you?"

"Bunch of lock picks and a switchblade," Sterling reported, sitting back in an armchair to preside over his pitiful prize.

"We can't go back empty-handed," Riley reminded them both, pushing her empty stomach to the back of her mind. "Not again."

Keith nodded in somber acknowledgment before sidling over to the window, fingering the weathered curtain aside and peering out at the street.

The former police officer had lost his beefy physique, his big cords of muscle having shrunken to ropey dense remnants after the series of long stretches in between their meager meals. He still filled out Nolan Armstrong's fur-lined leather aviator jacket, but only because it had been too tight for Keith to begin with.

Similarly, Sterling had turned from lean to gaunt, the ex-rancher now casting a stark figure in the loose folds of his green parka and camouflage trousers.

Even Riley had lost her slender frame – the only curve that she had left underneath her gray hoodie and jeans was her bloated belly.

A small part of her began to envy the pair of corpses in the living room. Their deaths must have felt like a sweet release, compared to the struggle of surviving on the edge of starvation each and every dreary desolate day.

"Something doesn't add up," she pulled her gloves back on as a thought occurred to her. "These two shouldn't have had *anything* on them. Who the hell's going around shooting people and not even stopping to at least check their backpacks?"

"Somebody who doesn't need to," Sterling shrugged, before tilting his head at the idea. "Maybe whoever killed these guys aren't that desperate."

"Or maybe they're just trying to protect what they've got," Keith stepped away from the window, looking at them both with renewed vigor in his stony gaze. "There's a stash in the house across the street."

"How do you know?" Riley asked, rising to her feet to peer between the damp curtains.

A brisk wind greeted her as it blew through the broken window, swirling frosty air across her face.

She didn't even know which house he was talking about.

They all looked exactly the same.

On the other side of the road was a row of identical double-story weatherboard homes, each one either lined with barren trees and bushes or leaning chain-linked fences.

This neighborhood looks like it was abandoned a long time ago, she thought to herself.

Windswept piles of broken glass twinkled in the pale winter sun.

Overgrown stalks of dead grass stood stubbornly over the

dusting of snow.

Tags of graffiti decorated most of the forgotten houses and cars – a parting gift from the first few waves of scavengers who had picked the homes clean.

A breath of winter blew again, wind whistling through the boarded-up windows of one double-story house across the street.

Riley furrowed her eyebrows as she glanced sidelong at Keith.

"You don't barricade an abandoned house," he finished her thought as he drew his pistol.

* * *

Continue reading on Amazon:
www.amazon.com/dp/B0BQZ9HF2G